Julia's
Mending

KATHY LYNN EMERSON grew up in Sullivan County, New York, where her family first settled in 1793. Many of the experiences in *Julia's Mending* are based on stories she learned from her grandfather, Fred "Scorcher" Gorton. Emerson, who now lives in Wilton, Maine, writes that "Grampa Gorton told me once that he wanted 'some noted writer' to use his life story as the basis for a book. I think he had Ernest Hemingway or John Steinbeck in mind, but I hope he'd be pleased with *Julia's Mending* too."

Julia's Mending

KATHY LYNN EMERSON

AN AVON CAMELOT BOOK

ACKNOWLEDGMENTS

Certain information in this book is based on the experiences of my grandfather, Fred "Scorcher" Gorton. I am also indebted to Pearl S. Buck's account of her mother's arrival in China in 1880 and to Emily Hahn's story of Nellie Bly's visit there on her trip around the world in 1889-1890. Julia's school resembles that described in Billie Gammon's *Norlands Schoolhouse, An Experiment in Living History*. Details of the apple-paring bee are drawn from the Sullivan County Historical Society's newsletter, edited by Delbert Van Etten. Rev. C. H. Wheeler's book is real. It was published in 1868.

AVON BOOKS
A division of
The Hearst Corporation
105 Madison Avenue
New York, New York 10016

Copyright © 1987 by Kathy Lynn Emerson
Published by arrangement with Orchard Books/Franklin Watts, Inc.
Library of Congress Catalog Card Number: 87-5793
ISBN: 0-380-70734-9
RL: 5.7

First Avon Camelot Printing: March 1990

CAMELOT TRADEMARK REG. U.S. PAT. OFF. AND IN OTHER COUNTRIES, MARCA REGISTRADA, HECHO EN U.S.A.

Printed in the U.S.A.

OPM 10 9 8 7 6 5 4 3 2 1

In memory of my father,
William Russell Gorton
1910–1986

Julia's Mending

⚘ CHAPTER ONE

Exile

"Lih-ber-tee Falls," the train conductor's rich baritone boomed. "Liberty Falls, next stop!"

Julia Applebee clenched her journal. So far it contained only today's entry, dated July 22, 1887. Julia gripped the small book so tightly that her fingertips made little pockmarks in its soft brown-leather cover. Almost there, she thought. Her heart began to beat faster.

"Your journey's nearly over, child," Mrs. Darbee reminded her.

Julia pretended she didn't hear her grandmother's elderly friend. Mrs. Darbee, on her way to visit her married daughter at the end of the line in Oswego, New York, had agreed to look after Julia as far as Liberty Falls. She'd laughed at Julia's plan to change trains at Weehawken and go on to California alone. "You're only twelve," she'd protested, as though Julia didn't know her own age.

I can't go back, Julia thought. Grandmama would never permit it. But there must be a way to go on. All I need is a little help. She watched the stout conductor thread his way toward them down the narrow aisle of the O&W passenger car. The bright gold buttons on his dark blue uniform threatened to pop off every time he drew breath to announce the next station. His face was red and blotchy. A line of sweat stood out in beads on his upper lip, above an enormous walrus mustache. Julia frowned. It's no good, she thought. He won't take me seriously either. He'll look at me and tell me that young ladies don't travel by themselves.

"Poor man," Mrs. Darbee murmured, her double chins quivering with every word. "That heavy wool uniform must be unbearable in this weather."

Unbearable, Julia repeated to herself. She turned away from Mrs. Darbee and stared out a window grimy with smoke from the steam engine ahead. Everything is unbearable! It's unbearable that I should be on this train at all!

The sultry summer weather added to her misery. Even the lace trim on her beautiful new traveling suit from Ghormley's, the smartest dressmaker in New York City, was limp and sticky. The long, dark green skirt felt pounds heavier than it had at the beginning of their journey.

She tried not to think about that. It was too painful to remember that Grandmama's last words to her had been a stern lecture. "Young ladies do not display emotion in public," she'd said. Julia had managed not to cry when they said good-bye, but if no tears showed on the outside, inside she had been sobbing as if her heart would break.

She could barely remember the ferry ride from New York City to the train station in Weehawken, New Jersey. It blurred together with her first hours on board. Then, gradually, she'd become aware of things around her—the hardness of the reclining chairs, in spite of their red plush upholstery; the constant shaking of the train as it swayed and jiggled its way north; the heat; the grime; and the rapidly changing countryside. There were no more city streets or brick buildings. As far as she could see, there were only miles and miles of fields and trees and small houses.

Julia clung tightly to her journal. It was the only link she had left with her mother, and the only sure means of escape from Liberty Falls. Unfortunately, it could not work quickly.

In the journal she meant to record her unhappiest private thoughts. Julia smiled at the blurry image of herself on the glass, and the brown-haired, blue-eyed girl smiled back. When it came time to exchange journals with her mother, Mama would see that it had been a mistake not to take Julia with them. She'd persuade Papa that it was time to send for her.

Papa had been very unfair. Not only had he and Mama gone off to be missionaries in China without her, but Papa had decided she could not stay with Grandmama in New York City either. He had exiled her to Cousin Lucy Tanner's farm in the country instead.

Grandmama's Washington Square townhouse was the place Julia thought of as her real home. During the last few years she'd gone to stay there every time her parents were busy with church work, and so she had spent more time with Grandmama and her maid, Alice, than with Mama and Papa. I'd be living there now, she told herself, if Papa hadn't heeded the "call." She wished he'd never heard of the Christian Missionary Alliance or their pledge to send twenty thousand missionaries out by the turn of the century. Most of all she wished he hadn't quarreled with Grandmama Pemberton over it. Grandmama did not want her daughter Louise, Julia's mother, to go to China. She'd told Papa it'd be enough to turn her off religion for good if they went. Papa'd promptly written to Cousin Lucy, and that was why Julia, in spite of her protests, was on her way to Liberty Falls in wooden passenger coach No. 65.

4

The trip from New York City had taken just over four hours so far. The train had stopped at dozens of stations along the route. Big towns like Middletown and Fallsburgh had seemed small and dirty to Julia, and the last stop, Luzon Crossing, had been little more than a wide spot in the road. Except for the time when she was writing in her journal, Julia had stared out the window at the unfamiliar countryside and brooded. She'd hardly said a word to Mrs. Darbee after that first, unproductive conversation. She was startled when the old woman spoke sharply to her.

"It's none of my business," she said, "but if you scowl too much, your face may stick that way. It would be a great pity. You've a few good features, you know. Your grandmother's cheekbones and your mother's pert nose. It's a shame you inherited Tunis's chin, but you certainly needn't stick it out in that stubborn way he does. Calls attention to it. Makes you look hostile. Not a good quality in a young girl." The train whistle sounded. It was long and loud and ear-shattering, but Mrs. Darbee kept right on nagging. "And don't purse your lips in a thin, hard line like that," she finished. "Look agreeable when you meet your cousins for the first time, and you'll find your new life much easier."

Julia forced herself to smile and thank Mrs. Darbee for her concern, but deep down she was

5

seething. Everyone claimed to know what was best for her, but no one ever asked her what she wanted. It wasn't fair!

They were thrown back against the cushioned seats as the engine jolted and jerked its way up to the wooden platform that served as a train station. It let out several noisy blasts of steam, then shuddered to a stop.

The hours on the train had crept slowly by, but now everything happened so quickly that it took Julia's breath away. Mrs. Darbee hugged her and wished her well, nearly smothering her in an ample, lilac-scented bosom. Then a uniformed porter helped Julia get her carpetbag out from under the seat and unloaded her trunk from the luggage car.

Abruptly, she found herself all alone. Cousin Lucy and her husband, Gil Tanner, were nowhere in sight, and no one else came forward to claim her either. Only an old yellow dog watched her arrival, and he was more interested in scratching a flea than in welcoming her to town.

I can't stay here, Julia thought. Her hands were sweating under her white cotton gloves as she looked in vain for another human being. She'd been told Liberty Falls was the nearest place to Cousin Gil's farm in Strongtown with a depot for taking on and letting off passengers. It should be a thriving community, teeming with life. Instead it was small and dreary and deserted at midday. She could see a few houses, one hotel, a schoolhouse, a store, and a black-smith shop. Not a single building rose over two stories high, and she had to look at them through a dismal gray haze. The air was full of soot from the engine.

"All aboard!" the conductor called, although there were no passengers waiting.

I could get back on, Julia thought, and hide. If I keep stowing away on trains going west, maybe I can even get to San Francisco before Mama and Papa embark. Then they'd have to take me along. She advanced two hesitant steps toward the train as it started to move. Her trunk was in the way. She'd have to leave it.

Julia's eyes stung. The train was moving faster and faster. More gritty cinders fell on her as it heaved a last steamy sigh and stranded her in a billowing cloud of black smoke.

🌿 CHAPTER TWO

Dreadful
and Beastly

Julia rubbed soot out of her eyes and peered hopefully toward the rest of Liberty Falls. A second store, the paint on its swinging sign chipped and peeling, stood on the other side of the tracks near a tannery, a grist mill, and two more houses. Nowhere was there any sign of life. She blinked. New York City had frame buildings, too, and unpaved streets and fields and empty lots, but it also had churches, department stores, and other enormous structures, like the Steinway piano factory that took up an entire block. Most of all, it had people, lots of them. Julia had spent hours watching them through the windows of Grandmama's townhouse and from the comfortable seats of her carriage.

The yellow dog yawned, curled once around, and went to sleep in the sun.

"Do you have an owner?" Julia asked it. She got no answer, but now a wagon was approaching the depot at a fast clip. She breathed a sigh of relief. Cousin Lucy at last! If she couldn't be with her parents or Grandmama, at least Cousin Lucy was family. Julia had been imagining her in a summer dress with a tiny waist, carrying a parasol and wearing a big hat with flowers on it. That was how she looked in the one old photograph Papa had.

"There she is," a plump, dowdy woman shouted from the high wagon seat.

That can't be Papa's cousin, Julia thought, but she knew in her heart that it was. She was no longer a slender young girl but a matron with six children, and she had not dressed up to come into town to meet the train. She wore a plain everyday dress that had once been a dark shade of blue but now had faded to a drab, unflattering hue. Julia could see dark stains under her arms as the little woman flapped a greeting. She flung herself down off the wagon, cheerfully bellowing: "Good old twelve twenty-two! Right on time!"

Lucy Tanner bounced up the steps, swept across the platform, and embraced her. "My favorite cousin's only daughter!" she cried. Julia stiffened at her touch, fearful of crushing her expensive dress, but Cousin Lucy didn't seem to notice. She went right on talking so loudly that the blacksmith came out of his shop to see what was going on.

"Why, you're nothing but skin and bones, child," she declared. "We'll soon fatten you up. Just you wait and see."

Julia didn't want food. She wanted a bath. She was filthy from the top of her tall feathered hat to the patent-leather tips of her new kid shoes. She wanted to soak in hot water and bubbles for at least an hour.

Cousin Lucy stood back and smiled at her. "Aren't you a sight for sore eyes! I'd have known you any-where, Julia Applebee. You've got your father's chin."

Julia couldn't think of a thing to say. She stared at a streak of flour on her cousin's shoulder, switched to a graying tendril of curly hair that had come loose from her bun, and finally met bright, relentlessly cheerful blue eyes.

"You'll get used to us," Lucy Tanner declared and hugged Julia again.

Cousin Gil hoisted her trunk into the back of the light lumber wagon. He was a tall, thin man, deeply tanned by the sun and sporting a bushy brown beard. His clothes were clean but as well worn as his wife's, and there was a patch sewn over one knee. "Best get a move on," he said. "Cows need milking."

"Your Cousin Gil has twenty-five dairy cows," his wife said proudly. "He's one of the most successful farmers around. He ships the milk to New York City on the train in great forty-quart milk cans in special milk cars."

She babbled on throughout the journey home, but Julia barely listened. She was wrapped up in her own thoughts. Liberty Falls had been bad enough, but the open countryside was worse. Houses were few and far between. To Julia, who had never been out of New York City before, this was wilderness. At first she expected wild Indians to attack at any moment. Then she became convinced that Cousin Gil was hitting every rut and bump in the dirt road on purpose to make her black and blue all over. Slowly and painfully they covered a mile and a half and then stopped in front of a plain white two-story house with a porch that ran the entire length of the front and turned a corner to connect to the attached shed. Nearby stood an enormous barn with a ramp leading up to large sliding doors standing open on its second level. A hay wagon still loaded with hay was just inside.

Julia stared. This couldn't be the Tanner farm. Papa had said Uncle Gil was prosperous. "Prosperous" meant brick houses three stories high, with flower beds in front and brass door knockers. Then she looked again at the rough work clothes her cousins wore. This was their house. She was going to have to live here.

"These are our children," Cousin Lucy said as five

ragtag figures appeared on the porch. "Simon, Grace, Daniel and David, and Jeanette. Angeline is just a baby, and she's inside."

Five pairs of blue eyes, the exact shade of her own, stared at Julia, unblinking. She tried to force her mouth into a smile, but before she could manage it the five-year-old, Jeanette, burst into speech.

"You've got soot on your nose!" she shrieked.

Julia felt her face getting hot. The rest of them stood silent, watching. Grace, who was nearest Julia's age, looked the least friendly of them all.

"Grace, show your cousin the way upstairs," Lucy Tanner said. "You two girls will be sharing a room."

Grace stomped inside, and Julia had to hurry to catch up with her. On the top floor she flung a door wide to reveal a tiny, crowded chamber with only one bed in it.

"We have to share that too."

Julia couldn't think of anything to say. She began to unpack, taking her underthings and dressing gown and slippers from the carpetbag. Grace, with manners that belied her name, showed her a single empty bureau drawer in which to put them. When Julia pulled out a cool, lime green muslin dress, Grace pointed sullenly at a rod stretched across the corner of the room. On it hung three dresses identical to the one Grace had on—an unflattering pale pink calico that faded her already fair coloring to a pasty white.

"There won't be room there for the clothes in my trunk."

Grace shrugged and took her own good time before she spoke again. "There's a *Kas* in my parents' room."

What on earth is a *Kas?* Julia wondered, but she was determined Grace shouldn't think her ignorant. Instead of asking, she announced, "I'd like to take a bath and change my clothes."

Grace snickered. "There's a tub you can use in the kitchen, but you'll have to heat the water for it yourself."

"In the kitchen? Where anyone can walk in?"

Grace nodded.

"Perhaps I won't bathe just now."

"Pretty fancy, aren't you? I hope you don't expect me to lend you my dresses just to keep yours clean."

Julia looked down at the soft fabric in her hands. It was too fine for country living, but she had other clothes in her trunk. "I don't wear hand-me-downs," she said and turned her back on Grace while she removed her dusty, travel-stained suit.

Julia didn't allow herself to think about a bath again until that night at bedtime when she took out her journal. She'd discovered on the train that it made her feel better to write about what was happening to her. Now, sitting beside a flickering kerosene lamp, she told the page (and Mama) how she longed to be clean again and compared herself to a prisoner serving a sentence for a crime he hadn't committed. That's good, she thought and went on to record that she thought Cousin Gil's farm dreadful and his children beastly.

She had been forced to spend a long, unpleasant evening with them. Except for Cousin Lucy, Julia didn't think any of these relatives liked her, although she couldn't understand why they wouldn't. Simon, the oldest, was a gangly, awkward boy of fourteen, who chewed straw and said little. Daniel and David, who were twins, talked constantly but mostly to each other and usually in incomplete sentences Julia found hard to follow. It was almost as if they had a secret language of their own, designed to keep her out of their conversation. Of the girls, Angeline was too young to talk at all, Jeannette plagued her with questions and rude remarks, and Grace hummed. Now, while Julia wrote, she was doing it again, repeating the same few notes over and over again.

"Do you have to keep making that noise?" Julia asked. "It's very annoying."

Grace didn't answer. Instead, still humming, she got up, gathered together some loose sheets of paper, tied them up with green ribbon, and said: "These are my private things. Nobody looks at them but me." She put the packet on the top shelf of a little bookcase. Along with the bed and bureau it was the only furniture in the room.

"And nobody looks at this but me," Julia snapped.

She slapped her journal shut with a loud smack. Then she tucked it into her carpetbag and slid the carryall underneath her side of the bed.

They didn't speak to each other again, although they lay side by side, awake, for a long time after they climbed into bed. Julia wondered what was so special about Grace's papers, but she didn't dwell on that mystery long.

I have no time to worry about Grace's secrets, she thought. It is much worse here than I ever imagined. I have to think of a way to get to China soon. She fell asleep dreaming up ways to convince Grandmama to change her mind, go against Papa's wishes, and send someone to the Tanner farm to rescue her.

❧ CHAPTER THREE

Through the
Pitch Hole

Breakfast was a silent meal. Julia began to wonder if her cousins were always so sullen. Their eyes followed every movement she made as she ate, as though they'd never seen a person with good table manners before. She was glad when they left the house to do chores.

Only Grace remained, and to get away from her Julia went into the parlor. She'd noticed the night before that a brand-new harmonium stood there. Now she saw, as she sat down at it, that it was a Mason and Hamlin "baby organ" just like the one at Grandmama's house. Grace followed her into the room.

"Grandmama's been teaching me since I was six,"

Julia said, exaggerating just a little. "How long have you played?"

The musical instrument was the first thing Julia had found in Cousin Lucy's house of which her grandmother would approve. Music wasn't Julia's favorite pastime, but she had begun to think there wouldn't be anything at the farm she could do. She knew she'd never be able to force herself to milk a cow, but she could play two pieces of organ music all the way through. The thought cheered her up, and she turned to look at Grace with a smile on her face.

"We only use the parlor for special occasions," her thirteen-year-old cousin announced. Her voice was fierce, and she screwed her face into an ugly scowl as she waited for Julia to come out. Then Grace closed the parlor door firmly behind them and stalked out of the house.

Julia's day passed very slowly after that. She spent most of it in the kitchen with Cousin Lucy. Julia was not used to kitchens. Once or twice she'd been in Grandmama's, to eat cookies fresh-baked by Rosa, the tall, skinny cook. At her parents' smaller house Mrs. Wilkins, the housekeeper, did plain cooking and sent out for breads and pastries. Mrs. Wilkins was very particular about her duties and wouldn't let Julia near. "You'll break somethin', dearie," she'd say and shoo Julia away. Cousin Lucy put her

17

to work, first shelling peas; then, after the noon meal, peeling and slicing apples. Grace and the other Tanner children had chores out of doors, under the blistering sun, helping their father.

At first Julia enjoyed the novelty of her tasks, but as the sultry afternoon wore on and the large nickel-plated cookstove continued to radiate heat, her long sleeves clung uncomfortably to her arms. She wondered if this was what Papa'd had in mind when he'd insisted that life in the country built character. If character meant getting red in the face and feeling wet and sticky, then Julia thought she could do without it.

Delicately wiping her brow with her cuff, Julia stole a look at Cousin Lucy. Her face was glistening with moisture too, but she didn't seem to mind. She chattered cheerfully on and on. If I hear one more word about cows or chickens, I'll scream, Julia thought.

"Why don't you have a hired girl to do the work?" she asked abruptly. Cousin Lucy's hands were wrinkled and crusty from housework, and Julia had begun to slice more and more slowly, fearful for the texture of her own. She already had a blister coming up where she'd been holding the small paring knife against her finger.

"Whatever for? That would leave me idle. Idleness encourages slothfulness, and slothfulness is a sin."

"Oh," Julia said and fell silent. Fear of sin had

never kept Mama from hiring help. It must really be, she thought, because Cousin Gil is too poor to afford help. He didn't have a hired man to help with the cows either. Her trunk, still holding most of her clothes, was stored in the nearly empty room in the barn where one should have lived.

"These are summer apples," Cousin Lucy explained, taking another from the basket that sat on the kitchen floor between them. "They are called Red Astrachans, and we have only a few trees because they lose their flavor within a day or two of being picked. They have to be eaten or cooked right away. Take a taste, Julia. Most of the trees in the orchard produce Baldwin apples. We'll harvest them in October."

Julia cut a slice out of the apple she had just peeled. The skin color varied from light to dark red, and now she saw that although the flesh was mostly white, there were red streaks in it too. "It smells good," she said as she lifted the piece toward her mouth.

It tasted delicious. Julia savored the treat. She'd never had apples in New York City until after Christmas. She supposed that was one advantage to living in the country. So far it was the only one she had found. She continued to nibble as she worked.

When all of the apples Julia had prepared were simmering on top of the cookstove, Cousin Lucy wiped her hands on her apron and said, "You've got an overheated look to you, Julia. Go outside for a breath of fresh air."

"May I go into the parlor instead?"

"The parlor? Whatever for?"

"I know it is only for special occasions, but . . ."

"Special occasions! Nonsense! Of course we don't go in there much as a rule, but ever since her father bought her that baby organ, Grace has used it regularly. No reason you can't."

Grace lied to me, Julia thought. I wonder why? Aloud she asked, "May I play the organ too?"

Cousin Lucy nodded absentmindedly. "Now where did I put that little hatchet?"

"Hatchet?"

"Yes, dear. I'm about to kill a chicken. I hope this one doesn't get too far once its head is off. They run in circles, you know, trying to escape when it's already too late. The last one went right into a thicket. Come along, Julia. That hatchet must be out by the woodpile."

"But I thought . . ."

"Oh, goodness me, child, you don't want to be in the parlor now! Even Grace isn't inside on a scorching hot day like this. Go join your cousins if you like. I can hear them down by the barn."

Reluctantly, Julia went. At least the shouting was well away from the henhouse and the bloody slaughter that was to take place there. She shuddered. She didn't think she'd be able to eat that chicken, now that she'd know how it died.

Julia's cousins were busy with a game of hop-scotch and paid no attention to her. She stood watching them for a long time, but not one of them invited her to join in. I don't want to play, she told herself. I don't want to have anything to do with them. Yet when Simon, with fourteen-year-old authority, glanced up at the sky and then hollered that the rain was coming, Julia ran with the rest of them for shelter in the barn.

They darted up the ramp and onto the threshing floor. She followed more slowly and was relieved to see that there were no animals housed on this level. Big animals had always frightened her.

Julia had never been inside a barn before. She glanced about her, curious, but she didn't have time for more than a quick look at the loft above and the farm equipment around the sides before Simon came at her.

An evil grin split his tanned, freckled face. Behind him, through the barn doors, Julia could see enormous black thunderclouds rolling in. As Simon moved closer, the sky grew darker and darker. The first loud crack of thunder sounded like a rifle shot. A moment later the whole barn grew bright as midday with a flash of lightning. Julia squealed and ducked, but it was too late.

A handful of dry hay cascaded over her head. It got on her hair and up her nose and in her ears and made her eyes water. Coughing and choking, she fought to brush it away. The dust made her sneeze, and the hay itself scratched her cheek as she pawed at it. It fell, sticky with sweat, to her white pinafore and left dirty streaks behind when she tried to flick it off.

She was mad enough to want to hit Simon, but she held her clenched fists tight to her sides. I will not give way to anger, she silently vowed. Young ladies of twelve and a half do not lose their tempers. Then Simon threw the second handful of hay.

"You devil!" she shouted at him. It was the worst thing Julia could think of to call him. She felt her face flush as red as the ribbon that held her hair in a long plait down her back.

Simon hooted with laughter. "Got you! You've been hayed!"

He scooped up another armload and aimed it at his sister Grace, but she was too fast for him. She hoisted her faded pink calico skirts, skipped through the door to the tack room and slammed it behind her. The ten-year-old twins, David and Daniel, crept up behind Simon and sent him sprawling face forward onto the barn floor. He bounded right back up. Hay clung to his scraggly blond hair, stuck out of the collar of his cotton shirt, and was even twisted through the braces that held up his denim trousers.

"Revenge!" he shouted and lurched toward the twins. His foot struck the tines of a pitchfork, flipping it perilously close to his head, but he only laughed and kept after them.

All four of Julia's cousins were having fun. Grace slipped quietly back out of the tack room and squatted behind the hay cutter, gathering up ammunition for a counterattack. Her unbound hair, so fine that no coarse-toothed comb could untangle it, flew into disarray with every move. She began to whistle a little tune as she launched herself at Simon.

Julia glared at her, wondering how she could be so unladylike. I will not lower myself to that level, she thought, and turned her back on her rowdy cousins.

No rain had started yet, though the barn had grown very dark inside. Julia heard another rumble of thunder, but this time it seemed farther away. Maybe, she thought, the storm is going to pass us by after all.

Slowly and deliberately, she picked the rest of the hay out of her hair and off her clothes. The soft red calico with its narrow white collar and plain wrist-length sleeves was not her favorite dress, but she didn't want to see it ruined. The skirt ended just above her ankles. As she brushed it, she sniffed. Sighing, she scraped the soles of her black leather bootees on the floor.

"I hate barns," she muttered to herself. This one

reeked of the cows housed on the level below her feet. She squinted, trying to see if there was another way out, and located what looked like a door in the side of the barn nearest the house. It seemed to her that if she left that way she wouldn't have to go within ten feet of Simon. Julia tossed her head to rid her hair of the last strands of hay and started off.

"Julia! Wait!"

She ignored Grace. Why should I listen? she thought. Grace made it plain the first moment we met that she resents having to share her room. And she lied to me about the parlor. Julia took two more brisk paces. Simon's voice reached her just as she stepped off into empty space.

"Look out for the pitch hole!" he shouted.

Julia felt herself falling and heard the sickening crack of bone against wood before everything went black.

CHAPTER FOUR

The Seven-Pound Weight

Golden dots twinkled. A flash of white blotted them out. Then Julia opened her eyes. She hurt all over. Her head pounded. Her hand stung from a long scratch on the palm. Her right leg throbbed. She could feel the rough, splintery wood it rested against right through her black stockings, and her first thought was that they were torn for certain.

Raindrops plunked steadily in the distance. Julia heard the grumble of thunder once more and waited for the lightning. She knew she was lying on her back in a pile of hay on a dirt floor in the basement of her Cousin Gil's barn, and in the brief flash of the lightning she could see the open space above her. She had fallen into the hole they used to pitch hay through.

Julia tried to push a strand of loose hair out of

her eyes. She regretted the impulse at once. Her stomach churned, and she thought she would faint from the sudden wave of pain. She didn't try to move again, but now the hurting wouldn't stop. Sharp twinges kept shooting from her ankle to her knee and back down again.

When the next lightning bolt flashed, Julia risked glancing from side to side. She discovered she was lying against a manger. Beyond it, from a stall with a nameplate marked "Lazarus," an enormous ox peered menacingly at her. Though there were solid planks between the girl and the beast, she panicked. She'd never realized how huge oxen were, especially when seen from the ground up.

"Simon!" she screamed. "Daniel! David! Grace!"

None of them answered. She couldn't tell if they were still in the barn or how long it had been since her fall. Outside, the patter of rain slowed to a drip. Finally, Julia heard faint sounds above her. A moment later four towheads appeared, framed by the pitch hole. As the storm passed over Strongtown and headed for New York City, it became light enough in the barn to see them clearly.

"Get up," Simon ordered.

"I can't get up," Julia shouted at them. "I'm hurt!"

Tears started to well up at the backs of her eyes. I want Mama, she thought. Never before had she felt so alone or so unloved. The shadowy figures above her blurred as she began to cry. Then they disappeared altogether. She sobbed harder, remembering that her parents had said they couldn't take her with them to China because they weren't sure it was safe. It seemed to Julia that the people in this "safe" place had left her to die!

She hiccuped and choked back her sobs. She refused to cry any more. It was a matter of pride. She was determined to be brave, but she wished with all her heart that Papa hadn't insisted on sending her to Cousin Lucy. He'd said, "We know what's best for you," but Julia didn't believe it.

If I ever get out of this barn, she vowed, I'll write to Grandmama and insist she come for me.

Cousin Gil crashed through a door at the end of the row of cow stalls. The sound startled Julia, and she turned, twisting her broken leg. She cried out in pain. Cousin Lucy's husband suddenly terrified her. He was a larger, dirtier version of Simon.

"Stop your noise, now," he said gruffly.

Julia shuddered as he reached down to pick her up, but he was surprisingly gentle. He lifted her until her leg hung limply and touched nothing but the soft inner folds of her petticoats.

It no longer seemed like a leg at all. It acted as if it had an extra joint in it. Julia winced. In spite of his care, Cousin Gil's passage to the house hurt. Each step he took increased her agony. There was no relief until he placed her on Cousin Lucy's soft feather mattress.

"Simon's gone for the doctor," Cousin Gil told his wife. "He's taken Major."

Cousin Lucy nodded and bent over the bed. Her cool, soothing hand felt under the thick fringe of hair covering Julia's forehead. "No fever," she said and smiled reassuringly. "Major is the fastest horse we own, but it's still three and a half miles to the nearest doctor, and if he is out when Simon gets there, it may be some little time before they get back. I'll have Grace sit with you until then."

Julia didn't argue. All she wanted to do was lie still. She heard Grace come into the bedroom but didn't look at her. This is all her fault, Julia thought. Hers and Simon's. They could have warned me about the pitch hole. They're probably glad I fell through it.

"Try to rest now," Cousin Lucy said.

Julia closed her eyes. She had already discovered that if she stayed perfectly still her leg didn't throb. Now she tried to make believe that she was back in Grandmama's house. Images formed one after another in her mind. There was the red brick house itself, tall and imposing on the tree-lined square. Then she wandered in her daydream through each of the dozens of rooms full of lovely furniture and paintings. She lingered in the one that had running water and a big claw-foot bathtub. That made Julia think of Alice, Grandmama's maid, who used to draw her baths for her. She dozed off remembering how Alice had been her first playmate.

The clatter of hooves woke her. For a moment she didn't know where she was. Then the pain in her leg reminded her.

It was dark and hot in the room, with the window open to the humid July air. Cousin Gil and Simon were just outside, as easy to hear as if they had been standing next to the bed. Cousin Lucy's bedroom was on the ground floor, and its windows opened onto the porch.

"Where's the doctor? You've been gone for hours."

"I came back as quick as I could. Did Ma save me any chicken? I'm hungry enough to eat . . ."

"The doctor, Simon—is he on his way?"

"First he was out," Simon said. "Then he refused to come. He recognized Major. He said that since you didn't like the way he set your wrist when Major kicked and broke it, he wouldn't set any more bones for you. Then, on the way back . . ."

"You told him it was for Julia? A little girl?"

"Yes sir, Pa. He said the only way he'd come was if you wanted an amputation done."

Julia drew in her breath. This can't be real, she thought. I must be having a nightmare.

"Hush, both of you." Cousin Lucy's voice snapped through the darkness. "Of all the foolish men! You're talking right beside the window. What if Julia's awake? You'll be scaring her to death."

"Sorry, Lucy." There was a shuffling sound in the gravel dooryard.

"Go in and have your meal, Simon. And you, Gil Tanner, you think on it tonight, and tomorrow morning you find another doctor, a good one. I never heard such foolishness! Amputate indeed!"

Julia closed her eyes and said a quick but fervent prayer of thanks for her father's cousin. "Lucy is a fine, upstanding, churchgoing Christian and she'll take good care of you," Papa had said. Julia thought how right he was. At least this awful place had one person in it who cared what happened to her.

It was the next afternoon before a doctor came. By then Julia was feverish and very scared. Dr. Hobart's appearance did not make her feel any better. He was dressed all in black, like an undertaker, and had a long, sorrowful face. Julia wasn't sure she wanted him attending her. She was still thinking about what that other doctor had told Simon.

While Cousin Lucy watched, the doctor took a look at Julia's leg. He felt the bones, gently probing with his fingertips. Julia winced. She couldn't bring herself to look.

"We'd better knock you out, my girl," Dr. Hobart said. "I'm afraid this will hurt a bit." He took a bottle of liquid out of his black bag and began to pour it into a handkerchief.

"You aren't going to cut anything off are you?"

He laughed without smiling. It was not a reassuring sound. "No amputations," he promised. "You'll be fit as ever in a few weeks."

The handkerchief came toward her face. In panic, Julia lurched away from it. The smell was sickly sweet.

Cousin Lucy was at her side, holding her down. "It will be all right," she said soothingly. "We won't let anything happen to you."

Julia did not trust the doctor, but she knew Cousin Lucy would never lie to her. Reluctantly, she took the drugged cloth from the doctor.

"Hold this to your nose," he said, "and count. You can count, can't you?"

"Of course I can. I passed the sixth grade this spring."

"Then start counting."

She could remember getting to thirty.

"She's coming around," Cousin Lucy's voice said. She was somewhere off to Julia's left. When her cousin moved, Julia knew she must be sitting on the edge of the bed.

In the background were the sounds of evening chores. One of the twins was chopping kindling for the next day's cookstove fire, and the cows were mooing. Nearer at hand the baby, Angeline, howled. Jeanette addressed her mother in her shrill five-year-old's voice.

"Is she dead?"

"No, darling. Just sleeping."

"What day is it?" Julia murmured. It seemed to her that months must have gone by. Her mouth tasted like sawdust, and she felt terribly, terribly heavy.

"Same day as before," Cousin Lucy told her. "Sunday, the twenty-fourth of July 1887."

Sunday? It didn't seem possible to Julia that she had only arrived in Strongtown on Friday. So much had happened.

Slowly, she opened her eyes. Her leg was still there, but she couldn't move it at all. From thigh to ankle it was in a wooden splint that looked like a big tray.

"Why is it so heavy?" she asked.

"There's a seven-pound weight hanging from your foot, over the edge of the bed. Dr. Hobart doesn't want you moving around until the break heals."

"How long will that be?"

"He couldn't say, but until you've mended, you'll stay right here in our room. Gil can sleep in the barn, and you'll share our bed with me. That way I'll be right here to help you if you need anything."

The baby cried again, and Cousin Lucy patted Julia on the arm and stood up. Jeanette, standing in the doorway, was swept along as Cousin Lucy left the room. Only then did Julia realize Grace was still with her, on the other side of the bed, sitting quietly on the window sill. She was mending a tear in Julia's red calico dress.

"You hollered louder than that when the doctor set your leg," she said.

"Grandmama says that a lady would never use that word out loud," Julia told her. According to Julia's grandmother, ladies didn't admit they had legs.

Grace shrugged and started to hum to herself. Julia frowned and wondered if Grace did that just to annoy people. The tune, if it could be called that, didn't resemble any music Julia had ever heard.

Still frowning, Julia surveyed her surroundings. The bedroom was bigger than Grace's but seemed as small because it was crowded with oversize furniture. Facing the bed was a painted pine-and-oak wardrobe—the mysterious *Kas*, or Dutch clothes cupboard—and to Julia's left a dresser and hope chest sat side by side. Behind them the wallpaper sported gigantic yellow roses, faded by the sun that streaked in through two windows on the opposite wall. A small table with an oil lamp stood between the nearest window and the bed. On Julia's other side the open door led to the rest of the house, but she could not see through it without twisting around in the bed, and that she could not do.

Julia glared at the heavy wooden tray that held her leg. I really am a prisoner now, she thought. Instead of shackles, I have a cast and a seven-pound weight holding me down. And I have Grace to torture me.

"Don't you have to milk Peanut?" she asked rudely. One of the twins had been teasing Grace about the animal, a short-legged cow Grace treated as a pet.

The humming stopped. Grace gathered her sewing together, her face hidden, but Julia could imagine the sour expression there. Soundlessly, she made her way around the wide brass bed and left the room. Julia's relief lasted only seconds. I should have sent her to her room to collect my things, she thought. I want my journal. Julia felt her features settle into a sulky scowl as she realized she'd have to wait until Cousin Lucy came back to send for it. She quickly put both index fingers to her lips and pushed the corners up. It wasn't that she believed Mrs. Darbee. Of course faces didn't get stuck. But she wasn't taking any chances.

❧ CHAPTER FIVE

Julia's Journal

Julia was alone for a long time after Grace left. At last she slept fitfully, coming fully awake only when Cousin Lucy entered the room with a glass of milk and some johnny cake on a tray.

"You've slept through the evening meal," her cousin told her. "Is there anything else I can get for you tonight?"

Julia didn't hesitate. She wouldn't put it past Grace to snoop through her things. "I'd like my journal," she said. "Mama gave it to me just before she left and made me promise to write in it at least once a week."

"Of course you shall have it!" Cousin Lucy exclaimed. "I understand about journals. I'll wager your mother is keeping one too, and you'll exchange them when next you meet."

"Sooner," Julia said. "We're going to mail them to each other."

Cousin Lucy brought back not only the journal, but Julia's photographs of her parents and the small, thick book, bound in red and black with gold lettering, that had been one of Papa's parting presents— Rev. C. H. Wheeler's *Letters from Eden; or Reminiscences of Missionary Life in the East.* The sight of it reminded Julia of something that had been nagging at the back of her thoughts all day. As far as she knew, no one but Cousin Gil had left the farm, and it was Sunday. Everyone had to go to church on Sunday. Julia blamed herself.

"I must have made everyone miss church this morning," she said. "I'm sorry."

"Oh, but you didn't."

Julia stared at her. "I don't understand. The church building didn't burn down, did it?"

Cousin Lucy laughed and explained. "When your father went to visit us, back when he was your age, my family attended the Methodist Episcopal Church in Strongtown, but I'm a Free Methodist now."

Papa didn't know that! Julia was sure of it. She was certain he'd not have sent her to Cousin Lucy if he had. He'd never had a single good word to say about the radicals who called themselves Free Methodists. Even leaving Julia with a grandmother who'd declared herself "off religion for good" would have been preferable to letting her come here.

Cousin Lucy chattered on. "A wonderful preacher named Reverend Thicket came through these parts in the spring and held a camp meeting near the schoolhouse. You never saw such shouting and carrying on! I nearly fainted myself, and Maybelle Potter, she fell right down in the middle of the aisle, overcome by the Spirit, and lay like a dead woman for five minutes. Didn't breathe at all. Then she stood up and jumped up and down and testified what the Lord had done for her and hollered 'Glory! Glory! Glory!' till she went hoarse. Well, by time it was over, Reverend Thicket had convinced me. I saw the error of my ways. From now on, salvation is free, and so are the pews. We've raised enough money to build our own church in Liberty Falls. It will be ready in time to hold Quarterly Meeting in it in December."

Julia felt like weeping. All this—the trip to Strongtown, the broken leg, the seven-pound weight —wouldn't have been necessary if Papa had been told in time. Now it was too late, and she was trapped. After Cousin Lucy took the tray away, Julia cried herself to sleep.

The next day she intended to write in her journal, but first, after breakfast, she composed a letter to her grandmother. It was difficult to keep her quill pen from going dry. Lying in bed meant she had to write up. She finished the letter with a four-square lead pencil Cousin Gil brought her, and she folded it carefully. By the time she got it addressed, her wrist ached almost as much as her leg did.

"Will you set my journal back on the table for me?" she asked him. "I can't write any more for a while."

It surprised Julia to find she liked Cousin Gil, even if he did have a faint barn smell about him. He was so tall he could reach across the bed from the other side to plunk Julia's journal down next to the lamp. He put her letter on top of the little leather-bound book.

"I understand all about diary books," he said. "I keep one myself to record when the crops are ready and what the weather is, and when I do special things like selling a horse or building a barn."

"Do you?" Julia couldn't help sounding surprised.

He nodded. "Stay put. I'll show you."

Where could I go? Julia asked herself. She couldn't even use the chamber pot without Cousin Lucy to unhook the weight and help her in and out of bed.

Cousin Gil wasn't gone long. He came back with a lined composition book like the ones Julia used in school and thrust it under her nose. "Here. Read that one."

The paperbound notebook had been marked off in Cousin Gil's big, curly handwriting with one date on each page. It was open to February 19, 1887.

"Bought a chestnut sorrel colt with two or 3 white

feet and a star on the head. He was coming 3 years old. Got him down to Sandburgh. $100. Named Major." Julia read the entry aloud and then looked up.

"That Major's one temperamental horse," Cousin Gil said. "If he wasn't so fast off the mark, I'd sell him."

"He kicked you and broke your wrist." Julia wasn't sure how she knew that. Then she remembered.

Cousin Gil looked embarrassed and hastily flipped to the last entry in his diary book. He pointed to the page dated July 25, 1887, and again Julia began to read aloud.

"Thomas Hicks had 2 cows and a heifer struck by lightning on July 23. They were standing under an oak tree. The same day Julia Applebee broke her right—" Julia stopped. She skimmed the rest of the entry in silence. "Julia Applebee broke her right leg by falling through the pitch hole from the barn floor to the basement floor and it was set by Doctor Hobart in the afternoon of the 24th."

Cousin Gil didn't notice her dismay. "That Major," he said. "Fool horse almost did Simon an injury too. The boy was in such a rush to get into town for the doctor that he didn't bother with a saddle. Coming back it was getting dark. Major stopped short and Simon pitched right over his head. Lucky he landed on his feet."

"Could someone mail my letter to Grandmama?" Suddenly Julia couldn't bear Cousin Gil's company any longer or any more talk of cows or horses or Simon.

"I'll send Simon up for it," Cousin Gil promised, "soon as he's done with chores. He can take it into town this afternoon."

Julia was dozing when he came. She pretended to be asleep and watched through half-closed eyelids as Simon went around the bed to get her letter. It was still lying on top of her journal on the small table to the right of the bed's glistening brass headboard. She couldn't see him pick it up, but she heard the rustle of the envelope and saw him go back the way he'd come to leave the room. Then she did sleep, secure in the knowledge that her plea for rescue was on its way.

When Julia woke up again, she felt better. She reached behind her and to the side for the journal. Instead she got the color picture book that belonged to Jeanette. It fell open to the little girl's favorite page, which had an illustration of a large dog. Underneath was a rhyme that read:

> We are singing, Floss. Be quiet now.
> Your song is only bow wow wow.
> You don't keep time. You cannot speak.
> We told you so one day last week.

So just wag your tail and hold your tongue
Until our pretty song is done.

Julia closed the book and set it aside as she fished again for her journal. Her fingers touched the smooth wood, then the frosted glass globe and brass stand of the lamp. With an effort, she twisted around to look. There was nothing else on the table.

"Simon," she muttered. Julia clenched her fists. He'd stolen her journal when he came for her letter. By now he'd read it. Julia couldn't remember ever feeling this angry before. Furious with him, that's what I am, she thought. If I could get out of this bed I'd throttle him with my bare hands!

She was about to call for Cousin Lucy and demand she get the journal back. Then Julia remembered what she had written in it. She didn't want to take the chance that Cousin Lucy might read those words. She'd meant them. The remarks about Simon had been kind compared to what she felt about him now, but for all that, Julia didn't want Cousin Lucy's feelings to be hurt.

She forced herself to calm down. Patience, Grandmama was always saying, is a virtue. Julia knew she had no choice. She would have to wait until she was able to hunt for the journal herself. "I know just where to start," she grumbled under her breath, "and if it's in Simon's room, I'll just take it back!"

✒ CHAPTER SIX

A Mystery

As an only child, Julia was accustomed to amusing herself, but the days passed very slowly. Of all her young cousins, only Jeanette visited her, and that was Cousin Lucy's doing.

"Why don't you read aloud to her?" she suggested. "It will help you pass the time."

After the first week Julia felt as if she could recite the whole of Jeanette's picture book by heart, both forward and backward. She longed for *Little Women* or *Heidi*, but she had not brought any of her own books to Strongtown. She'd foolishly supposed Cousin Lucy would have a library, as Grandmama did. Cousin Lucy had just one book, the Bible her parents had given her when she got married.

The only other book in the house was Reverend Wheeler's memoir. Julia put off reading it as long as she could. She was honest enough with herself to admit that she'd wanted to accompany her parents to China solely because she loved them, not because she shared their calling to be missionaries. Secretly, she thought Grandmama had been right when she told Mama to her face she was plain crazy.

At last, however, Julia picked up Reverend Wheeler's book and started to read it aloud to her five-year-old cousin. It was as boring and goody-goody as she had feared and soon drove Jeanette away. To keep the annoying little girl from bothering her, Julia kept reading.

Two slow weeks went by. Julia saw Cousin Lucy when she brought her meals and at night, but she rarely talked to anyone else. She tried to tell herself she preferred things that way and that she didn't like her cousins any more than they liked her, but she couldn't help feeling left out, especially when she detected the faint sounds of the organ in the parlor and knew that Grace was playing. She'd sigh then and tell herself it didn't matter.

Julia pinned great hopes on her letter to Grandmama. Soon, she told herself, Grandmama will send someone to rescue me. Meanwhile, she passed the time by thinking of all the things she'd write in her journal when she got it back, by sleeping many extra hours, and by forcing herself to read the rest of Reverend Wheeler. She found the book, especially the last chapter, hard going. Julia knew she fell far short of living up to the author's ideals, and she didn't like having it pointed out to her.

The final chapter had a list of requests. Reverend Wheeler asked his readers to keep the book clean and take particular pains not to tear the map. That was the easy one. Then he asked them to do all they could for the cause of missions—by earning and giving money to send the gospel to heathen lands, by prayer, and by considering doing mission work themselves, if they went for the right reasons.

Julia frowned down at the page. I don't care what you say, Reverend Wheeler, she thought, I'm going to China to be with my parents!

She turned the page. He had one more request. Last of all, Reverend Wheeler wrote: "Do all the good you can to those about you."

Julia set the volume aside, face down. "You ask too much, Reverend Wheeler," she whispered aloud. She wished she could be selfless like her parents, but she knew she wasn't. What she wanted most right now was a letter from them, telling her where to meet another missionary family and come after them. It would be a while before letters started to come. China was so far away that Papa and Mama hadn't even arrived there yet.

Papa had said she should read their letters aloud in church, she remembered, so that people would know of the good work being done and support it. Julia produced a long-suffering, shuddering sigh to equal any her grandmother gave forth when Papa began to preach the rewards of missionary work.

"I won't do it," she vowed under her breath. "I won't share my personal letters with strangers." Then she smiled. Maybe I won't have to, she thought. Now that Cousin Lucy has defected from the Strongtown Church and Grandmama has stopped attending services altogether, I may be able to keep my letters to myself. The possibility made Julia happier than she had been for weeks.

Dr. Hobart reappeared the next day to remove the traylike cast. He still reminded Julia of an undertaker, but at least this time he smiled. It had been just three weeks since Julia's fall. Dr. Hobert replaced her cast with bandages, wound round and round until they were at least an inch thick, and promised that they would soon come off too.

"Why, the last case I had like yours," he told her, "the young lad was out running in the orchard, bandages and all, when I came back to remove them."

Julia experimented, cautiously, after the doctor left. It was still awkward to move about, but she could get out of bed by herself again, and manage the chamber pot without Cousin Lucy. She could also hop around the room.

A few hours later Julia hopped over to the window to see what all the commotion was about in the dooryard. Lace curtains covered Cousin Lucy's windows, and through them it was possible to see without being seen. Cousin Gil was unloading the light lumber wagon. He had brought home six piglets, and everyone was making a huge fuss over them.

It was nearly evening when Cousin Gil knocked on the door. "I've come to stop all the noise about the pigs," he said, gruff-voiced.

"What noise?" Julia bridled at his tone. She hadn't said a word about the pigs.

Cousin Gil put his arm under hers and helped her limp out to the pig sty. "The twins haven't let up for a minute. They say you have to pick out a name. Angeline is still a baby. The sixth piglet is for you."

Propped up against the sty, Julia had no choice but to look down on the squealing black piglets. Their antics made her laugh in spite of herself.

"That one's mine," Simon said. "I'll wager there'll be more bacon and ham out of him than any of the others." He had a silly smirk on his face.

"Ham?" Julia looked puzzled. "What do you mean?"

Grace arrived at the pig sty just in time to hear the question. "What do you think we keep pigs for?" she asked scornfully. "Pets? The fattest one we slaughter ourselves. The rest we sell to the butcher."

"The best one we ever had weighed two hundred eighty-five pounds," Cousin Gil boasted. "Back in 1878. Sold the pork at six cents a pound."

Julia felt ill. This was worse than the chicken. "I don't want one," she said. "I don't care about any old pigs! Please take me back inside."

They were all staring at her, looking surprised by the fuss, but after a moment Cousin Gil did what she asked.

Julia bit her lip as he placed her gently back on the bed. Her leg throbbed a little, but that was not the real cause of her pain. No one liked her here. She was more convinced of it than ever.

She was sure that this whole scheme to give her a piglet was a plot to make her feel stupid. She *had* thought they were pets, and she'd have liked a pet. Julia felt sorry for the poor little pigs who were destined to die. She couldn't understand how anyone could raise an animal without growing attached to it. Didn't they feel like cannibals every time they ate ham?

Julia rolled over on the bed. The movement brought her eyes level with the table, and she sat up in surprise at what she saw there. Her journal was back! It had been returned.

Until she'd touched the soft brown leather, Julia was half afraid she was dreaming, but the book was real. She plucked it from the nightstand and began to write. She had to catch up on three weeks of entries. Industriously, she penned an account of all that had happened to her, but even while she was recording how miserable she felt, another part of her mind was puzzling over the mysterious return of the little book.

Who had brought it back? Had she been wrong about Simon after all? He hadn't been in her room today. And she hadn't left it, except to go look at the pigs, and he'd been there with her, was still there for all she knew.

If Simon didn't return it, she asked herself, who did? There were only two possibilities, Grace and Cousin Lucy, but she couldn't imagine why either one of them would have taken it or why they should have waited so long to bring it back.

❧ CHAPTER SEVEN

Scorcher

The next morning, Julia was moved back upstairs into Grace's room. Just before noon Cousin Lucy paid a visit.

"I don't know what to make of you, Julia," she said as she came through the door.

Julia looked up in alarm. Had her cousin seen the journal after all? But the plump little woman made no mention of it. She sat down on the edge of the bed and took Julia's hand in hers.

"We all know you miss your parents and your grandmother, and that you are hurting from the accident, but if you want to mend and be whole again, you have to make an effort. Feeling sorry for yourself never mended anything."

She took a deep breath that shuddered its way all

around her ample form when she let it out, and plunged on. "Today you start coming to meals with the rest of us again, and there are plenty of chores you can help with around the kitchen. It's better to be busy than idle, I always say. Takes your mind off your troubles."

Julia didn't have any choice. With her cousin's help she descended the stairs and hobbled to the kitchen. Grace was tending a big pot of chicken and dumplings on top of the cast-iron cookstove. The table, covered with oilcloth, was set for the meal, with plates and knives and forks at each place.

Julia couldn't help herself. She was thinking of Grandmama again, comparing all this with the way meals were served at her house. Grandmama had two tablecloths covering the big oak table in the dining room at every meal, white linen on the bottom, and lace on top. There were linen napkins too, held in silver rings, and finger bowls at every place. In Strongtown everyone washed at the hand pump next to the sink, lathering up with strong lye soap.

"Where's Simon?" Cousin Gil asked.

"I sent him into Liberty on his bicycle to the cobbler's shop. The twins need half soles on their leather boots again. He'll be back soon."

"He won't miss a meal," Grace said.

"He's the fastest rider in town," Daniel chimed in, pushing a lock of hair back out of his eyes. "They call him Scorcher."

David nodded vigorously, shaking an identical lock up and down. "He can get from here to Liberty in eleven minutes. And that's three and a half miles."

Tires scraped to a halt on gravel with a shower of small stones, and Simon appeared in the kitchen door. "Fastest trip yet," he declared.

"Anything new in town?"

"Not much, Pa." Simon washed his hands quickly and came to the table. "Got a letter for Julia though." He drew it out of his shirt and handed it to her. The envelope was smeared with dirt and sweat.

"I do hope the writing inside hasn't run!"

Julia's sarcasm was lost on him. He merely shrugged and started stuffing food into his mouth.

Cousin Lucy frowned at them both. "Read it after we eat, Julia. Now then, young man, when does Mr. Liebman say the boots will be ready?"

"Next week."

She nodded. "Good. The twins can pick them up."

"We can walk into town?" David asked.

"By ourselves?" Daniel finished.

"I think you two are old enough now. I'll give you each five cents to spend as you see fit."

"Marbles!" David decided. "I can get ten for a nickel."

"Candy," Daniel said firmly. "Or gum."

"Saw the Hardy brothers," Simon said. "They're in big trouble. They got some blasting powder at the blacksmith's shop and put it in the anvil in a hole three inches square. They covered it up and set it off and were so tickled with the bang it made that they did it again. The second time a spark must have been left in the hole, because when they put powder in the third time, the anvil exploded and Hank's eyebrows got burned right off. He sure looks peculiar."

David, who sat next to Julia at the table, explained for her benefit. "Their mother says they're a mite careless. It must be true. The other brother, Fred, has two fingers missing. He caught them in his father's ice cream freezer."

"They knead the bread dough for the bakery with their bare feet," Daniel added.

"I almost had an accident coming back," Simon said. He kept on shoveling dumplings into his mouth as he talked. "I was scorching along near the stone bridge when a cat ran right in front of me. I was going so fast I couldn't stop. I ran right over it."

Julia gasped. The others kept on eating.

"Is it dead?" Jeanette asked, her mouth full of chicken.

"Naw. It was sitting up and shaking its head. I looked back over my shoulder."

Julia stared at him in disbelief. "Didn't you stop?"

"And ruin my chance at a new record?"

"How can you be so heartless?" Julia realized with horror that she was shouting at him, but she couldn't stop. "How could you just go off an leave a wounded animal? You terrible boy!"

She got up and left the table, unable to eat any more. She wanted to run back to her room but the bandages slowed her down. A shambling gait worked best, half hopping and half dragging her bad leg. It seemed to take an eternity to climb the stairs. Julia hugged the letter from her grandmother close to her as she stumbled along, praying it contained instructions to return to New York by the next train.

Safe in the bedroom under the eaves, Julia took the letter out and started to read. Her eyes misted over. This couldn't be right. She wiped at them angrily and read the brief message again. Grandmama wasn't in New York anymore. She hadn't even gotten Julia's letter. This note was to say that she had closed up the house in Washington Square and taken a ship to Europe. By now she was almost as far away as Julia's parents were and might be gone for months.

Julia stared at the letter for a long time. She had never felt so miserable in her life, not even right after her fall. Worse, she couldn't cry. She had cried too much in the last weeks. She had dried up.

She started to stuff the note back into its envelope, resisting the temptation to tear both envelope and letter into tiny pieces. That was when she saw the other sheet of paper. It was folded, and on the outside Grandmama had written: "I was hard on your father. I found this in some things he left to be given to charity. It's proof even Tunis was young once, a good thing for both of us to remember."

The paper was a hand-drawn map. Across the top, in block letters, a boyish hand had written LOST INDIAN LEAD MINE. Julia stared at the words, then turned the paper first one way and then the other, hoping to spot some landmark, like the railroad tracks or the Tanner farm. Hard as it was for her to imagine her father as a boy, she knew that he had spent his summers right here in Strongtown. Cousin Lucy had lived on a farm a mile or so to the south. It had been sold after her parents, Julia's father's aunt and uncle, died and had been, so Cousin Lucy said, standing empty the last year or two.

This mine must be near the old Applebee farm, Julia thought. I wonder if I could find it? She had no idea if lead was a valuable treasure or not, but she was excited by the prospect of hunting for it.

Soft tapping noises at the door interrupted Julia's musings. She looked around for a place to hide the map. The best she could do before the door opened was to tuck it under her pillow, out of sight.

The twins hesitated in the doorway.

"You may as well come in," Julia said reluctantly. She didn't really want company, but she didn't suppose she had much choice, and at least the twins hadn't done anything to her. Compared to Grace, who had lied to her, and Simon, who had probably stolen her journal, and Jeanette, who was a very rude little girl, they had almost been friendly.

Both faces wore identical grins, wide and toothy, and they walked close together, both holding their hands behind their backs.

"We brought you something," David said. Julia could tell it was David because he had a small scar near his temple.

"Do you want to see it?" Daniel asked.

Julia nodded. She couldn't help smiling back at them. They were so obviously pleased with themselves about something.

Daniel turned his back on her and reached behind his brother. Around their stocky little bodies, Julia caught a glimpse of color and movement. "It's the cat Simon hit," he said, and held out a small, furry calico kitten, wide-eyed with fright.

The kitten lay very still in Daniel's hands. Its left front paw was hanging limply, bloodstained, and its nose looked as if it had been damaged too. Julia felt tears spring to her eyes as she reached out and took the injured feline out of her cousin's hands. She couldn't think of a word bad enough to call Simon.

"We went back to the bridge and looked for her," Daniel whispered. "She'd dragged herself home, to the old Steenrod place, but Laverne Steenrod, she didn't want to bother with no hurt cat. We said you'd take her and nurse her. Will you, Julia? Ma says it doesn't make no nevermind with her."

"Of course I will." She was already examining the little animal's wounds. The kitten's fur was very soft and beautifully colored, dark for a calico but liberally spotted with brown and red, cream and black. There was one black foot and three white ones. Carefully, Julia felt the injured black paw. "It's broken, I think. Do you know where I can get some small pieces of wood? I can make a splint."

The twins were gone and back in a flash. They watched, fascinated, as Julia duplicated on the cat what the doctor had done to her. The animal seemed to be in shock and hardly moved until Julia was done. The only response then was a weak meow as Julia gently wiped the cat's face.

"Look!" she said with a laugh. "What I thought was an injury is only the odd color of the fur. The kitten's mouth has a circle of light brown all around it."

"It's a girl cat," David said. "Ma said so."

"You get to name her."

For a moment Julia was reminded of the piglets, but she told herself that was silly. This was a pet, a real pet, and she would give the little cat a name. Jo, perhaps, after the heroine of her favorite book.

"You ought to name her Lefty," Daniel said.

Julia looked up from her new charge in surprise. "Why?"

"Because she's hurt her left foot. Even when she gets well, she'll favor her right."

"Then it ought to be Gimpy!" David made the suggestion, but both twins laughed.

Julia had to look away so that they wouldn't see her face. The cat was not the only one who might have a permanent limp. Will they start calling me Gimpy too? The thought chilled her.

"She needs something to eat," Julia said aloud. She forced herself to sound more cheerful than she felt. "Milk, I think. Do we have any?"

Again both twins laughed, but this time Julia laughed with them. She had completely forgotten the Tanners had dairy cows. "Silly me," she said and smiled her first genuine smile in weeks. "Will you bring a saucer here?"

The cat drank thirstily and then curled up as best she could with her bandaged leg and went to sleep. Soon after, the twins lost interest, crept out, and left Julia alone with her new charge.

"You and I have a lot in common, Lefty," she told the sleeping cat. The name came out naturally, and she didn't suppose the cat minded. It was better than Gimpy. "We both were injured because Simon Tanner doesn't care who he hurts."

She stroked the soft fur, finding it soothed her to do so, and presently she heard a loud purring begin. At least you like me, Julia thought. It felt good not to be alone any longer.

She was about to tickle Lefty's soft underbelly, which she had just discovered was an unlikely pure white, when a rustle from the doorway arrested her movement. Grace was watching them. Julia could not tell how long her cousin had been standing there, but she suspected she had been overheard conversing with a cat. Grace probably thought her a fool. Julia's eyes snapped and her fists clenched as she rounded on Grace.

"Have you come to make fun of the cripples?" she demanded.

Grace stared at them in silence for a moment longer, then went away. Julia could hear her begin to hum her odd little tune as soon as she reached the stairs.

✣ CHAPTER EIGHT

Head Cock of the Roost

Two weeks after Lefty's rescue, school started in Strongtown. Carrying her lunch in a pail, Julia limped after her cousins. The bandages were gone, and she could walk normally again. She'd been confident she could make the trip to school without help, but now her leather bootees pinched her feet, and the injured leg had begun to ache. She felt as if they'd been walking for miles but still saw no sign of a schoolhouse.

"Why don't we go to school in Liberty Falls?" she asked Daniel. "It must be closer."

Daniel was the only one who'd noticed she was lagging behind. He waited patiently for her to catch up while the others went on ahead. And why, she added to herself as she reached him, couldn't we ride in the wagon?

"But, Julia," Daniel protested. "Liberty Falls is a quarter of a mile further!" He fell into step with her and eventually announced that Strongtown School was just over the next rise.

"Thank goodness!" she exclaimed. Then she got her first glimpse of the building. "That's it?" She felt like crying.

Daniel nodded, then sprinted ahead when a dark-haired boy waved at him from the schoolyard.

Strongtown schoolhouse was a small wooden building at the intersection of two roads. It had been painted bright red. Julia could guess what she was going to find inside—one room, one teacher, and no indoor plumbing. She limped down the last hill, glumly aware that her lips were set in a thin, hard line and her chin thrust out.

The schoolyard held a half dozen children ranging in age from eight to thirteen. Together with the five oldest Tanners and Julia, that brought the school's enrollment to only twelve. Julia stood alone at the gate, watching them greet each other, all old friends. No one came near her. There was only one other girl near her own age, and she was whispering with Grace. Julia could guess who they were talking about.

"That's Nan West." Daniel suddenly reappeared at Julia's side, his dark-haired friend in tow. "This is her brother Racie. He's our best friend."

"Racie?"

"Short for Horace."

When Daniel and Racie stayed at Julia's side, she began to feel a little better. From the day Lefty came into her life, Julia had felt the twins liked her. She was equally certain that Simon and Grace did not.

"Are your sister and Grace best friends?" she asked Racie.

"They are now, but last year it was Simon who was always with Nan. They'd play 'Horse' every nooning."

"Horse?"

The boys nodded. David joined them in time to hear Julia's question.

"Haven't you ever played?" he asked.

"I've never even heard of the game. It must be a country pastime."

"It's fun!" David objected.

"Don't feel bad, Julia," his twin said. "It's just because you went to a girl's school before. You have to have boys to play 'Horse'."

Racie nodded, and she recognized pity in his look. "A boy takes the bit in his mouth or a line under his arms and a girl 'drives' him. Simon runs faster than any of the other boys, so Nan nicknamed him 'Black Beauty' after a horse in a book she read."

Julia couldn't imagine it. Simon pretending to be a horse? Simon being nice to a girl? Impossible! She looked around the schoolyard for her oldest cousin and found him standing alone, staring at two figures who were rapidly approaching the schoolhouse from the east.

"Who are they?"

"I never saw them before," David told her.

The boy was about Simon's age. The girl was much smaller, almost as tiny as Jeanette.

Julia watched their arrival with great curiosity and a sense of relief that she was no longer the only new student at Strongtown School. That boy is nice-looking, she thought, except for his scowl. All of the boys wore shirts with detachable collars, ties, and jackets to school, but this one had on a Sunday suit, complete with a vest and pocket watch.

The newcomers didn't say anything to anyone, but the new boy and Simon glowered at each other. They were as wary as two strange dogs meeting for the first time.

Julia began to inch her way forward. If no one else can be friendly to these strangers, then I will, she decided. The sharp jangle of a hand-held school-bell checked her in midstride. She turned, startled, and then stopped and stared at the open schoolhouse door. Her impulsive gesture of friendship was forgotten. The teacher was a man!

Julia had never had a man teacher before. This one was tall and skinny and had a prominent adam's apple. He was wearing a black, single-breasted worsted suit with a blue waistcoat, in spite of the heat of the day, and when he put down the bell he pulled out his pocket watch.

"You have two minutes," he said, "to file into the classroom and take your seats. There will be no talking."

In respectful silence, wary of the only adult in their midst, the pupils formed two lines. Julia, pushed to the front of the girls' line, was the first one to go in. She stopped in the doorway to make her curtsy. This was something her lady teachers had always insisted upon, but Julia discovered it wasn't done here. Grace bumped right into her.

"Keep moving!" her cousin whispered.

They've no manners in Strongtown, Julia grumbled to herself. She passed into the schoolhouse. Grace and Nan were right on her heels, trying unsuccessfully to stifle their giggles.

"New patent seats," Grace whispered.

"Watch out for splinters!" Nan's words were mixed with more giggles.

The inside of the schoolhouse was as bleak and unappealing as Julia had feared. The walls had clapboard wainscoting halfway up and plaster above. They were bare except for one small wooden blackboard. Benches had been pushed against three sides of the room, and the patent seats were arranged in rows, two on each side of the wood stove. There was a long stovepipe that went to the back wall, designed to keep all of the heat from the stove in the building. In front, next to the door, was the teacher's desk, an old lift-top with a lock.

The oldest pupils sat at the back, and Julia quickly chose a desk and untied her packet of school supplies. She had a slate and slate pencil, a quill pen, and some of Cousin Lucy's homemade brown ink. It smelled nice and reminded her of maple syrup. It was made, Cousin Lucy had told her, from the bark of swamp maples. Julia also had copies of Noah Webster's spelling book and a reader.

The girls stood by their desks until the boys had entered. Simon and the newcomer had to take desks next to each other at the back, on the other side of the stovepipe from Nan, Grace, and Julia. The two boys, who stood fidgeting behind their seats, were almost exactly the same height, but while Simon was fair and gangly, the other was dark and heavy set. They still hadn't spoken to each other.

The teacher tapped his ferule on his desk. "Straighten your rows," he said. Only when that was done did he address them with a solemn "Good morning, scholars."

"Good morning, Teacher," fourteen voices answered in unison.

"Scholars, be seated." He waited until they settled down, glancing at his watch to hurry them along. "My name is Mr. Raby, and I will be your schoolmaster this term. I will now call the roll. You will answer by saying 'present.' "

Julia didn't try to remember all of the names, but she did take note of the new boy's. It was Charlie Kilbride, and his little sister was called Hattie.

"We will begin school promptly at nine every morning and end at four in the afternoon," Mr. Raby went on. "You will have an hour's nooning. Every morning will be taken up with reading, writing, and arithmetic. The afternoon session will begin with a story, followed by your recitations in geography and history. Any of you who lack a copy of Mr. Smith's geography book must purchase one from Mr. Manion's store in Liberty Falls. He sells them for sixty-seven cents. Following recitations, the older scholars will learn grammar and the younger ones, if they have finished their lessons, may play quietly at their desks. I recommend that any spare moments be spent pondering the motto of the day."

He pointed to the blackboard. On it he had written the words "Fortune favors the resolute." Julia read it and winced. I don't believe it, she thought. If resoluteness alone would do it, I'd be on my way to China now!

"The last recitation each day will be spelling," Mr. Raby continued. "All scholars will line up with their toes touching the same crack in the floorboards and take part in a spelling bee based on Mr. Webster's book. There will be time saved at the day's end to clean the schoolroom. I expect you each to have your own small rag with which to clean your slate, and a blotter for spatters from your quill pen. You may provide yourselves with rocks from the schoolyard on which to sharpen your slate pencils. I will provide the large cloth with which to clean the blackboard. One student each morning will be selected to do that chore and also to sweep the floor, carry in kindling and wood for the stove, and draw water for the copper water container here in the entryway. There will be no spitting in the tin dipper."

Julia had stopped listening to Mr. Raby. Every time his pacing form turned away from the boys' side of the room, a glint of light shot out from that direction. The new boy, Charlie, was using a looking glass to watch the girls across the room. Grace and Nan started to giggle just as Simon reached over and grabbed the small mirror. At the same moment Mr. Raby turned around. He was down the aisle between the rows of desks in two long strides. He jerked Simon up out of his seat by the collar and pinned him against the wall. Simon never knew what hit him.

"I don't hold with such behavior in my schoolroom," Raby shouted. His face got red and his adam's apple bobbed.

Simon tried to speak, but Raby was nearly choking him. By the time the teacher had manhandled him back into his seat, the boy had stopped trying to protest his innocence.

The whole incident was all over in a matter of seconds, but its effect lasted the rest of the morning. No one dared do anything but listen attentively to the teacher.

Julia was glad when nooning came at last. She wished she didn't have to go back inside at all, but she meant to enjoy what time they did have out of doors. She sat down under a tree with the twins to eat her lunch. It was cornbread smeared with jam.

"Where are we going to get sixty-seven cents for that book?" Daniel complained.

"Where do you think? Pa'll make us take it out of our chore money."

"Chore money?" Julia asked. "Do you get paid for doing chores?"

"Some," David told her. "Not the regular chores, like chopping wood, but the extras. And we can earn more working for other people if there's time after Pa's satisfied. One year we built rabbit traps out of old boards, and sold the rabbits to Joe Sanford for ten cents each. Then, when the season was over, we sold the traps too, five of them, to George Crispell for fifty cents."

"We?" his twin protested. "You couldn't saw a board off straight! Me and Simon did all the building."

David grinned. "Share and share alike, that's Pa's motto. He made us split the money three ways."

"That isn't very fair," Julia said.

The twins exchanged glances. "Once," Daniel told her, "Simon spent eight hours holding bags while buffalo feed was shoveled into them from a railroad car at the switch at Strongtown Crossing. The railroad boss asked him if fifty cents was enough to pay him, and Simon almost had his hand around the money. But Pa'd overheard, and he came up and told the boss that twenty-five cents was plenty for a boy of Simon's years."

Julia wasn't quite sure what buffalo feed was and wasn't about to ask, but she had the strong feeling Simon had deserved as much pay as he could get. "That wasn't fair either," she told the twins.

Daniel shrugged. "Pa don't want to spoil us."

" 'cept Grace," David put in. "Pa bought her that organ so she could learn to play her tunes proper."

Julia frowned. She didn't think Grace had been near the parlor since the day Julia was moved back into her room. She knew she hadn't heard Grace playing. How odd, she thought. She was about to ask David to tell her more about Grace's tunes, but he was no longer at her side. He'd finished his lunch and disappeared.

"Where'd he go?" she asked Daniel.

The remaining twin pointed. Across the road from the schoolhouse was a stone wall four feet high. David and Racie were placing a plank over it to use as a teeter-totter, and a moment later David was teetering with Daisy Dodge.

"Are you going to desert me too?" Julia asked.

He nodded. "We'll get up a baseball game pretty quick. David and Racie and me and Wilbur Bennett —he's eleven like Racie—and the little boys, Alvin Hicks and Ned Lane. Simon too, I guess. Last year the older boys wouldn't let Simon play because he'd step out of line and try to hit every pitch."

"Older boys? What happened to them?"

"Finished school. Simon's head cock of the roost this year."

"You mean there are no schools with higher grades?"

Daniel shrugged. "Could go to Liberty Union School, I guess. But why would anyone need more than eight years of school?"

"Is it the money?" Julia asked. "Surely there must be scholarships for poor boys."

Daniel looked startled, but before he could answer her he was distracted and sprang to his feet. "They're going to fight!"

Julia looked up in time to see Simon round on Charlie Kilbride. Charlie, who was bigger than Simon, laughed in his face and leveled one quick punch at Simon's chin. He dusted his hands and walked away before Mr. Raby appeared.

"I fell," Simon insisted when the teacher saw him lying in the schoolyard.

No one contradicted him.

⚕ CHAPTER NINE

The Gauntlet

"That was well recited, Julia," Mr. Raby said. "You may be seated."

Julia was pleased with herself. It wasn't often anyone received praise from this teacher. She smoothed the layers of serge dress and calico pinafore on her lap and pushed back a strand of light brown hair that had sprung loose from behind her ear.

"Stuck-up teacher's pet!"

The whisper came from near by. Julia ignored it. Grace, she thought, or Nan. They're just jealous. Besides, she argued silently, it isn't entirely my fault. I can't help that I already know most of the recitations Mr. Raby asks us to memorize. I can't very well unlearn them!

Julia chewed thoughtfully on her lower lip. Knowing them and showing off a little hadn't made her any more popular with her classmates. She wondered if she could improve things by poking fun at the teacher. No one liked Mr. Raby. Soon after school started, he had the nickname "the rabid dog."

"Old Raby looks a lot like Ichabod Crane," she said as Nan and Grace walked past her that nooning. It was mid-September, and the two friends were looking for colored leaves to press between the pages of their schoolbooks. The maples had just begun to turn.

"Who is Ichabod Crane?" Nan asked.

"You know—the schoolmaster in Washington Irving's 'The Legend of Sleepy Hollow.'" Nan had lots of books at home. Julia had been sure she'd be familiar with the story, but Nan didn't know it, or said she didn't, and no one else had read it either.

Julia turned and walked away from them. Not even the twins wanted to be with her anymore. They were off playing baseball with their friends.

Lefty is my only friend, she thought. She and Grace slept every night in the same bed, but they might as well have been miles apart. Grace never spoke to her cousin unless she was forced to.

Simon presented a different problem. He'd finally started talking to Julia, and now she wished he hadn't. He'd be sure to come up behind her during the walk home this afternoon and mimick Mr. Raby's whining voice: "Well recited, Julia. Go to the head of the class, Julia." So far she had managed to ignore him. Papa always said that was a better way to deal with bullies than by getting angry. They'd get bored, Papa said, and go away. Julia hoped Simon was going to get bored soon. Maybe he'd start to pick on Charlie instead. Charlie earned Mr. Raby's praise in class, too.

Julia had been writing down all of her troubles in her journal. Soon it will be time to send the book to Mama, she thought, staring bleakly at the trees that surrounded the schoolyard as she ate her lunch. The wind began to blow, turning up the leaves until their pale undersides showed.

She wished that wind would blow her all the way to China. She longed for the day when her parents would send for her and she could leave Strongtown for good. They had never said how long she was to stay, but she knew she was trapped for at least as long as it took for the journal to reach China and a letter to come back. And then, she wondered, what will the letter say? What if they decide to leave me behind forever?

As the pupils began to file back inside the school after nooning, Mr. Raby suddenly appeared in the doorway, blocking their way.

"You girls will remain outside," he announced. "I have something to discuss with the boys."

For once Nan and Grace acted together with Julia. They moved in unison to listen at the window.

Mr. Raby's nasal whine reached them clearly

through the leaded glass: "I understand there is a rumor going around, a very nasty rumor, concerning myself and one of the girls. It has been said that I was seen coming out of the girl's privy. That is no crime. But one of you added, without a grain of truth, that I was in there at the same time as a student, Miss Julia Applebee."

Julia gasped, glancing quickly from Grace to Nan. They were torn between giggles and horror, which made Julia suspicious. Had they already heard the rumor? She didn't have any doubt at all about who had started it. It was exactly the sort of thing Simon would do.

One by one, Mr. Raby questioned the boys. Daniel and David knew nothing and said so, and the others all pretended to be innocent whether they were or not—all but Charlie.

"Simon repeated that story to me," Charlie said. "I didn't believe it, of course."

"He did not!" Grace's whisper was agitated. "Simon doesn't even speak to Charlie, not ever."

In spite of Julia's certainty that Simon was to blame, she also believed Grace. Charlie and Simon had avoided each other like the plague since the first day of school.

Julia hadn't said much to the new boy either, though at first she'd wanted to. She'd thought about making friends with him when Cousin Lucy told her that Charlie's family was living at the old Applebee place. Julia had been poring over Papa's map again and had decided that one of the landmarks on it must be Cousin Lucy's old home. She'd have asked for Charlie's help to find the mine if she hadn't secretly feared he'd take the map away from her and look for the treasure on his own.

Inside the schoolhouse there was dead silence. Simon didn't say a word. The girls leaned closer, to hear what Mr. Raby was doing. Suddenly Jeanette's shrill voice broke the spell: "What are you looking at?" she shouted from the other side of the school-yard. Then Mr. Raby was at the window, and all three eavesdroppers were caught.

He marched the boys outside to join them. "It is only fitting, now that you girls know what is going on, that Julia, who has been so wronged in this in-stance, be allowed to watch the punishment meted out to the one who wronged her. Simon will run the gauntlet three times and spend the rest of the day locked in that outhouse he is so fond of gossiping about, and if there is any further trouble I'll pay a call on Gil Tanner."

Julia didn't understand at first what running the gauntlet meant. When she did, she was shocked.

"Oh, no!" she cried out. "I don't want Simon hurt!" She didn't want to have to watch either, but no one paid any attention to her protests.

"We won't really hurt him," Daniel whispered as he passed her.

Julia wasn't sure she believed him. She watched with growing alarm as the boys lined up in two rows. Simon was to run between the rows while they hit him with their fists, but Julia saw both sticks and stones being secretly gathered too. She couldn't look after the first run. She held her hands over her eyes, but she could still hear the thumps as blows fell on Simon's body. He stumbled once, too, and almost fell, when Charlie cracked him sharply on the back of the ear. Julia saw that through her fingers.

"Oh, please stop!" she whimpered. She wished she had courage enough to run forward and fling herself between Simon and his tormentors, but she didn't.

At last it was all over. Grace glared at Julia, plainly blaming her for everything. Simon wouldn't look at anyone as he walked to the outhouse, but his face was a bright, ugly red. Julia sensed his humiliation and feared he hated her more than ever. The twins didn't know how to act. They'd joined in the gauntlet with a will, but Simon was, after all, their brother. They avoided Julia too. That really hurt.

Julia could not concentrate on schoolwork after that. She kept thinking of poor Simon, and the more she thought about him, the more unfair his punishment seemed. She even began to wonder if he had started the rumor. There was only Charlie Kilbride's word for that. By the end of the day she had worked herself into such a state that she actually confronted

Charlie. She followed him when he ducked behind the schoolhouse and was just in time to see him stuff a monstrous quid of chewing tobacco into his mouth.

"Why did you lie about Simon?" she demanded.

"I never lie," he mumbled as he began to chew, cowlike. He walked away, but Julia followed. She had to run to catch up, and they were out of earshot of the schoolhouse before she could.

"How do I know that?" she panted, grasping his arm to make him stop. "Nobody knows whether you'd lie or not, but you are a bully. And a snitch. And chewing tobacco is a disgusting habit!"

Charlie laughed and spat tobacco juice. It came within an inch of Julia's bootees. She stepped back in alarm, then, chin quivering, drew herself up to her full height and pointed. "Look at that puddle," she said, indicating the tobacco juice on the ground. "A filthy toad wouldn't get into that! What if the tail of my dress dragged through that muck? I don't understand how a boy of your years could pick up such a nasty habit!"

"My uncle chews," Charlie mumbled and spat again. He was looking at her with interest, as if he was curious to see what she would do next.

"Filthy tobacco chewer! I hope you turn green and gag on the entire wad of it!"

She picked up her skirts and swung away from him, just in time to see Simon start down the road

76

toward them. She couldn't make out the expression on his face. He was too far away.

"Coming to see if you fought his battle for him," Charlie taunted.

"He's coming to make sure I'm all right!"

Julia hoped that was it. Simon might just as easily be looking for revenge. When he changed his mind and retreated in the direction of the schoolhouse, she followed, refusing to look at Charlie again. He may have Mr. Raby fooled with his nice clothes and his scholarship, she thought, but not me!

To her relief, Simon hadn't waited for her. All of the Tanners were on their way home, leaving her to trail along after. Was he worried about me? she wondered and was surprised to realize that she hoped so.

❧ CHAPTER TEN

Simon's Dilemma

After Simon ran the gauntlet, Julia's journal entries began to change. She still wrote about how lonely and miserable she was, but as she wrote, she began to think about what she was saying. I sound like a spoiled brat, she thought. I haven't been letting myself look beyond the end of my own nose.

Simon shouldn't have read my journal, an inner voice complained, but Julia answered herself: You shouldn't have been so quick to call him names and insult his way of life.

It took her almost a week to argue everything out in her head, but once she had, she knew that she owed Simon an apology. The fact that he had been avoiding her only made her more determined to make amends. A week to the day after he had run the gauntlet, she waylaid him on the way home from school. Simon's four siblings were ahead of them on the road.

"Go away," he grumbled, glowering at her, but Julia stood her ground.

I've gone on far too long with no one to talk to but Lefty and the twins, she thought. I not only want to be friends with Simon, I want to be friends with Grace. Neither one of them can really be as awful as they seemed at first. Her tentative attempts to talk to Grace had been coldly snubbed, but Julia wasn't giving up, and in the meantime she was determined to have more luck with Simon.

It was as much my fault as theirs that we didn't get off to a better start, she reminded herself. I didn't give a single thought to whether my cousins wanted a stranger living with them or not. I selfishly thought only of my own misery and expected everyone to spoil me and pamper me the way Grandmama and Alice did. With horrible clarity Julia could now see every mistake she had made with her cousins, and she regretted each one bitterly. They had plenty of reasons to think her stuck-up and unfriendly.

Julia matched Simon's pace, though it made her leg ache to walk that fast. I'll stick to him like a burr until I've apologized, she vowed. She cleared her throat. She knew she was doing the right thing, but that didn't make it easy. They had come abreast of a walled-in one-acre lot full of apple trees. Abruptly,

Simon veered off. He was carrying a twelve-foot-long fishing pole, a bait can, and a lunch pail, but he managed to get a toehold in the five-foot wall and clamber over.

"Simon!" Julia wailed. "I want to talk to you. It's important."

He didn't answer. Julia stared at the wall, torn between her grandmother's ideas on ladylike behavior and her own single-minded determination to apologize to Simon. She took a deep breath, tossed her head, stuck out her chin, and scrambled up the wall after him. She had dropped off the other side before she realized that the lot was occupied. There were three cows and a bull inside, their curious gazes fixed on the two intruders. Julia tried to ignore them. Simon was already halfway to the far side. Gathering up her red calico skirts, Julia began to run after him. Behind her she heard the bull bellow and begin its charge.

Simon turned, startled by the sound, and saw Julia for the first time. His eyes widened but he didn't panic. "Hurry," he shouted. He waited for her to reach him.

Julia expected to be gored at any moment. Her heart was pounding, and her breath began to come in short, painful gasps as she ran for all she was worth. Ignoring the pains in her newly mended leg, she reached out for Simon, trusting him to find a way to escape. Then she had to run even faster as Simon caught her hand and pulled her after him toward the far wall. They reached it only seconds ahead of the bull. Julia stopped short. The wall was lower than the one on the other side, but too high for her. I'll never make it over in time, she thought. Not with this leg! I'm going to die! Then she saw Simon's pole and lunch pail fly past as he tossed them over the wall. The next moment he had stopped to pick Julia up in his arms. She felt herself swept into the air, then sailing over the wall. She crashed into a soft, gently rustling pile of leaves on the other side. A second later, Simon landed in a heap next to her. The bull, close behind them, stuck his head over the lowest spot in the wall and bellowed again.

Julia and Simon looked at each other. Suddenly they both started to laugh. They were still laughing as they picked themselves up, dusted each other off, and started walking home again.

"You're limping!" He sounded concerned.

"It's nothing. It's from the fall in the barn."

He looked embarrassed. "I didn't notice before that you still limped."

"It doesn't matter. You just saved my life."

He shrugged, his face reddening even more under his freckles. "Aw," he said. Then he frowned. "Why were you following me anyway?"

"I wanted to talk to you. I owe you an apology."

He was amazed. "For what? I did start that story about you and old Raby."

"You didn't deserve to be beaten up that way."

He shrugged. "Is that what you wanted to apologize for?"

"No. It's something else."

They walked a little way along the wall until they came to a spot where Julia could sit on a boulder and rest her leg. She rubbed the new bruises on her ankle, staring down at her boot so she wouldn't have to meet Simon's eyes. She was not proud of the things she'd written about him.

"I'm sorry for what I put in my journal the first day I was here. It was unfair and unkind, and I don't blame you for being mad at me about it."

He was quiet for so long that she looked up. The expression in his clear blue eyes was puzzled.

"How could I be mad if I haven't read it?"

"But you must have!"

"You aren't talking sense, Julia."

She stared at him. He was the one who wasn't making any sense, unless he really hadn't read her journal. "But," she stammered, suddenly unsure of herself, "if you didn't take my journal, who did?"

"Let me get this right. Someone took your journal? When?"

"The day you mailed my letter to Grandmama. That's why I thought you had it."

"It was there. I remember picking up the letter from on top of it. I was curious, but I didn't peek. Is it still missing?"

"No. It was put back while I was out looking at the pigs." She felt herself reddening. "I was awful that day. I didn't understand. I thought you were trying to make me look stupid."

"Why would we?"

"Well, I thought you'd read my journal. I wrote some terrible things the first night I was here. I was so mad at my parents for making me come here that I took it out on all of you."

Simon helped her get up and balanced her while she tried her weight on her bad leg.

"I blamed you for my fall too, which wasn't anybody's fault, and for being heartless about Lefty, and you weren't. Daniel told me you were the one who sent them back that day, to look for the cat and bring it to me as a pet."

He shrugged a third time. "You were right. I was cruel to leave her there. She might have died."

They walked the rest of the way back to the farm in silence, but as soon as Simon entered the house he spoke up. "I want to know who borrowed Julia's journal," he told his brothers and sisters, "and I want to know now."

They all stared at him, puzzled, except for Grace. She gave Julia a startled glance before her face became carefully blank. Then Cousin Lucy turned from the table, wiping her flour-covered hands on her apron. "Has it gone again?" she asked.

"Again! You mean you knew it was missing before?"

"Oh, dear." Cousin Lucy looked flustered. "I'd hoped you hadn't noticed. I found it in Jeanette's toy box. She must have taken it for a storybook. I just put it back on the table by the bed."

"It was gone for three weeks," Julia told her.

"But my dear, why didn't you say so? We would have hunted for it and found it I'm sure. Jeanette didn't mean any harm, you know. She just loves books."

"It isn't important," Julia mumbled. She couldn't stop staring at Grace. What, she wondered, was the reason for that odd expression? It had flickered across Grace's features at Simon's question, coming and going so quickly that no one but Julia had noticed it. She couldn't describe it, yet it had convinced her that Grace knew more than she was letting on about Julia's journal.

"Mystery solved," Simon said, and he winked at Julia when he could catch her eye again.

Her answering smile was weak. Simon didn't take the journal, she thought, but Grace is still a suspect. Maybe she hid it in the room Jeanette shares with Angeline after she read it. Why else would she still be acting so unfriendly toward me?

"Simon, dear," Cousin Lucy said. "There's a letter on the table you should see."

He picked it up, glanced at it quickly, and scowled. "Ma!" he protested.

"Don't be hasty, Simon. Go somewhere private and read it, and search your soul. You'll see I'm right."

With ill grace, Simon slammed out of the kitchen and headed for the barn. Julia hesitated only a moment, then followed him. They were friends now, and he acted as if he needed a friend.

The barn no longer frightened Julia. Gradually, over the weeks she had been in Strongtown, she had gotten over her nervousness around the oxen, Lazarus and Ike, and made friends with Major. She didn't even notice the cow smell as she went and stood by the hay hole, looking down into the area that housed the animals. The pile of straw had been replenished. It was used, she'd learned from Daniel, for jumping into. It had been just bad luck she'd hit her leg on the manger pole that day. Even more ironic, the door she'd been headed for wasn't a door at all but opened on a sheer twelve-foot drop to the ground below. It was used for a hoist.

She looked around for Simon, but found Lefty first. The small calico cat was staring intently into a crack, looking for mice. She was strong and well now and had less of a limp than Julia did. She'd begun to put on weight too, the result of her attacks on the mouse population in the barn. Cousin Gil said she was the best mouser he'd ever seen.

Julia reached down and picked her up. "Come on, Lefty. Talk to me. Where did Simon get to?"

"Hsssst!"

The sound came from over her head, from the loft above the threshing floor. She looked up, gasped in alarm, and dropped the cat. A horrible face leered down at her, black and shiny with two slits for eyes. She opened her mouth to scream, and shut it again when Simon's face appeared from underneath the mask.

"It's just a piece of black oilcloth. I didn't mean to scare you." He was grinning.

"I wasn't scared."

He laughed, but his mirth had a friendly sound. "Come on up," he invited.

Awkwardly, Julia climbed the ladder to the loft. Simon was burrowing under a pile of hay. "Why are you hiding it?"

"I don't want the twins to find it. Oops! Here comes the band. Get your head down."

Grace came into the barn, humming loudly. They stayed very still until she left again. Julia's thoughts remained on the mask.

"What are you going to do with that horrible thing?"

"Keep it secret?"

"I promise."

"Remember what old Raby said about any more trouble? He'd come here if there was any? Well, I'm planning to give him some."

"But why? Your father will thrash you if you act up at school."

"It'll be worth it."

Julia couldn't imagine anything worth getting hurt for and said so, but Simon shook his head. He reached into his shirt, pulled out the letter his mother had urged him to read, and passed it silently to his cousin. It was from a seminary in Chile, Pennsylvania. They advised him to finish high school and then apply.

"I don't understand," Julia said. "Do you want to be a minister?"

"Sometimes you're very thick. Do you really think what we want matters to our parents? Ma's convinced herself I'll make a preacher. She's got her heart set on it. She even picked out the seminary!" He took the letter back and crumpled it savagely.

Julia had to agree with Simon. She could not imagine him as a minister. "You've got plenty of time to talk her out of it," she pointed out. "It says right there that you can't get into the seminary until you finish high school."

"I don't even want to start high school. But Ma's

got that figured out too. Next fall I'm to ride my bicycle to Liberty every day. They'll let me go to the Union School for five dollars a term."

"I thought Cousin Gil was too poor to send you boys on to school."

"Where did you get that idea? Pa favors education. And he's got plenty of money in the bank."

"But he makes you pay for your own school-books!"

"That's why he's got money in the bank." Simon grinned. "Anyway, I'm not going. High school is a waste of money. Ma can't see that now, but she will. She will." He fell silent, chewing a long piece of straw.

Julia began to mull over what he'd told her, but the realization of what he meant to do soon drove all thought of how wrong she'd been about Cousin Gil's frugal ways out of her head. "You're plain crazy, Simon Tanner!"

He just grinned. "If I act up enough in school, Raby'll complain to Pa. Now Pa may favor education, but he's not crazy about this seminary idea. He doesn't belong to any church and swears he'll die the way he's lived if it kills him."

"If he's not set on you becoming a minister, isn't that enough? Won't he put his foot down with Cousin Lucy?"

"Ma's pretty determined, and Pa don't like to stand in the way of anything she wants. I'll have to keep acting up long enough to convince even Ma that I'm beyond redemption. Then she'll give up on making me a preacher."

"But Simon, you'll get a reputation as a trouble-maker."

He shrugged. "Don't matter."

Julia wasn't so sure, but she couldn't think of any way to convince him that "acting up" was a foolish way to get what he wanted. "Where does the mask come in?" she asked.

"Not sure yet. I'll think of something."

Julia sighed. Now that they were friends, Simon's dilemma became her problem too. She decided to try to think of a way to persuade Cousin Lucy to give up her plan, without Simon getting into more trouble at school. After all, she thought proudly, I've already done the impossible once. Simon and I are friends.

❧ CHAPTER ELEVEN

The Lost Indian Mine

The next day at nooning Julia headed Simon off. "Where are you going in such a rush? I've got something to tell you."

He grinned. "Thought I'd talk to Charlie."

"Simon Tanner—you mean to pick a fight with him!"

Simon just kept grinning.

"Simon, I've got to tell you something," she repeated. Fighting was not part of her plan, and besides, she needed his help. "There's a lost Indian lead mine nearby, one Papa knew about when he was a boy."

"Indian lead mine?" Simon's brows lifted into two skeptical arches. "Julia, everybody knows somebody who used to have a map to a lost Indian mine."

"But I have a map now! Grandmama found it in

Papa's things. If you help me, we can find it. I think one landmark is your grandfather Applebee's old farm, where Charlie and Hattie live now."

"Are you sweet on Charlie? Is that why you don't want me to fight him?"

Astonishment left Julia speechless for a moment before a flood of words burst forth. "Sweet on him? I don't even like him! He's the most disgusting boy I've ever met! He even chews tobacco!"

"So does half the county," Simon pointed out, "and the other half is wondering what you're squawking about."

"That doesn't make it any less disgusting." Julia lowered her voice and glared at Nan and Grace until they stopped staring at her.

"Let me see your map."

"Wait." The baseball game had started, the teeter-totter was out, and the older girls had lost interest in Julia and Simon before she would take the carefully folded paper out of her reader and hand it to him. A slight breeze rustled the page as he opened it and stood studying it in the bright sunlight.

"You'd think you had a map to a Blackbeard's treasure," Simon complained. "Finding lead's not like striking gold or silver or diamonds. This probably isn't even a lead mine. Your map's more likely to lead to an old cave. There are lots of them around. There's one near the riverbank where a crazy man stayed forty days and forty nights. While he was there, he read the Bible right through and was cured."

"Even if it is only a cave, I want to find it. Please, Simon, help me look for it?"

"I don't know if I can." He was turning it this way and that to figure out where the places on it might be. Julia had the sinking feeling he'd rather be fighting with Charlie.

"You can do it, Simon."

He grunted. "It's a carefully drawn map. Cousin Tunis put a lot of work into it." They pored over the sketch together. Trees were etched in and rocks, flowers, and ponds; but there were no houses shown, and Julia couldn't begin to guess which roads or streams the many crisscross lines referred to.

"I think this might be the crossroads we're at right now," Simon mused. "See that little hill? I think it's meant to represent this one." He pointed at the rise of land just in back of the schoolhouse.

"When can we hunt for the mine? Is there time now, or tomorrow at nooning?"

He frowned. What was he thinking? She wondered if he believed he owed it to her to help, to make up for the story he'd spread about her and the teacher. She hoped not. She wanted him to agree because they were friends. She was about to say so when he answered.

"Tomorrow," he promised.

* * *

It was easy enough to slip away at the start of nooning the next day. Mr. Raby generally left the children to their own devices. As long as they were back in their seats when he rang the bell, he didn't care how far they roamed.

Simon and Julia climbed the hill behind the school as if they were going to picnic at the top, and then struck out in the direction indicated on the map. It's a perfect day for treasure hunting, Julia thought. The trees had almost all turned color now, and the rich reds of the maples contrasted with the yellows and golds of the other trees.

"I was right," Simon said, and pointed. "Eight hemlock trees. I'm surprised they're still here. They'd make nice logs to go to the sawmill. Hemlock timber is worth twenty dollars per thousand feet."

"I wish I could tell one tree from another," Julia said.

"Not hard. The big one in the schoolyard with all the initials carved in the bark is a beech." As they climbed, he pointed out a chestnut, a hickory, and a black cherry, and everywhere were the apples, their fruit bright red and almost ready to pick. "Every Arbor Day," Simon told her, "each of the older pupils transplants a tree to the schoolyard. Last year I planted a spruce as tall as I was next to the woodhouse. I named it Benjamin Franklin. Nan's tree was Martha Washington and Grace's was

Thomas Jefferson. Mine's the only one that thrived. In the spring I dug up some wildflowers and transplanted them, dirt and all, around the trunk of my tree to landscape it."

He fell silent as the going became rougher, offering her his hand to help her along. There was no path, and the ground was rocky and uneven. Julia had to grit her teeth several times to keep from crying out when her foot slipped on the rough terrain. Then she forgot all about her stiff leg.

"Look!" she cried. "The forked tree!"

It was the second landmark, and it meant they really were on the right trail. A few more minutes of brisk walking brought them to a third sign, a stand of birch trees; after a sharp right turn they soon spied the fourth and final marker, a split rock.

"It should be right here," Julia said, disappointed. She peered into the crack in the giant boulder. A small animal might nest there, but the gap could never be mistaken for a mine.

"You don't think it's right out in the open, do you?" Simon looked as hot and tired as she felt, but as her enthusiasm waned he seemed more intent on succeeding in their quest. "Look at those rocks." He was pointing beyond the single boulder to a rockfall on the side of the hill.

"I don't see anything special about them."

"They aren't flush with the hillside. I'll bet there's room to squeeze behind them or climb over them and, if the map is right, they hide the entrance to the mine."

Together Julia and Simon scrambled up the steep incline and edged their way through the large rocks. It was a tight fit at the last, but they made it. They stood together, out of breath, in a tiny hollow. Underbrush grew up all around them in the small open space between the rocks and the hillside. Simon studied the shrubbery with care.

"See that indentation," he said. "There's your mine." He began to tear at the bushes. This time they did find an opening into the earth. It was small and low to the ground, but it was definitely an entrance.

"We'll have to get down on our hands and knees and crawl to go inside," Julia complained. "And it looks dark in there."

"We'll come back with a lantern or candles. It's a cave, but it could be a mine too. We won't know until we go inside."

"Do you think it's worth anything? I mean if it is a lead mine, could somebody mine it and make money at it?"

He shrugged. "You need lead for bullets, but there must be plenty of it around, and there isn't even a war going on anymore, not since Geronimo and the Apaches surrendered last year. This mine probably hasn't been worth mining since there were Indians living around here."

"When was that?"

"The only Indians in these parts were the Lenape, and they've been gone for a hundred years."

Julia's respect for Simon went up. He might not do well in school, but he knew a lot of things she didn't. "What do we do next?"

"Nothing for now. It's our secret. We don't say a word until we have a chance to come back and explore the whole thing."

Julia felt as pleased as if they'd just discovered gold. "Our secret," she repeated. They sealed the bargain by shaking hands.

They had to rush to get back to the school on time, and the slight limp that still plagued Julia slowed them down. Partway there, when Simon paused to let her rest, she had the odd sensation that they were being watched. She looked up at the rocks just in time to see a dark shape pull back. Julia stared at it. It might have been some woods animal, but just for a second it had looked like a person's head. She called to Simon, but it was too late. Whatever it was had disappeared, and they had no time to go back and investigate.

The next day was Saturday, the first day of October, and they had chores to do. Cousin Lucy had kept her promise to keep Julia busy, but by early afternoon both she and Simon were free. Armed with candles, they returned to the hidden mine. Julia was surprised to discover that it was easier to come directly from the Tanner farm than to start at the school. Now that he knew where it was, Simon took the direct route.

"Ready?" he asked as they stood once more before the concealed entrance.

"Ready." They got down on their hands and knees and crawled in, candles held carefully out in front of them. Julia's nose wrinkled in distaste. There was a peculiar smell inside. She inched forward carefully until the space opened up enough to allow her to rise.

"It's not a mine," Simon said, looking around. It was, as he had first suggested, no more than a hidden cave. "Still, it can't be found until you're actually upon it, and that makes it a good secret place."

Julia smiled, sharing his sense of satisfaction. It was large enough inside the cave, at least in the middle, to stand upright without bumping her head. Julia did not venture further. The smell was stronger here, and it was very dark outside the two small circles of light their candles made. She let Simon explore the depths alone while she watched and listened. Hidden away inside the cave, she could still hear birdcalls and other sounds from outside, but they were distorted by the stone walls around her.

"There's a draft from somewhere," she said. Her candle was flickering.

"There may be another entrance, smaller, some-where above you. If there is, we could have a campfire in here if we wanted to and heat this cave up as snug as a house."

"That would be nice," Julia said. It felt chilly in the cave, for no sunlight reached inside to warm it.

"Watch out!" Simon shouted.

Julia started toward him. "Have you found something?"

Before he could answer, both candles blew out. Julia had only a quick, terrifying glimpse of the reason. There were bats at the rear of the cave! She flung her arms over her head as dozens of the tiny mammals surged past her, agitating the air in the cave with their wings. The horrifying sound filled her ears, and Julia felt a strand of her hair caught and pulled as the onslaught continued. Shaking with fear, she kept her eyes tightly closed until the last vibration of sound faded and she was certain that the bats had all fled.

"Julia? Are you okay?"

Her candle had fallen and been lost. She reached for Simon's hand in the darkness, half afraid she might touch something else. She grasped it thankfully, feeling the calloused fingers with a sense of relief.

"Bats," he said. "It's a bat cave." He was shaking with silent laughter.

Julia was still scared. "We've got to get out of here! They aren't waiting for us, are they?"

"I don't think so. Most wild critters are more scared of us than we are of them."

"Speak for yourself!"

He chuckled and pulled her along after him. Slowly, they crawled toward the lattice of light at the cave's brush-shielded entrance. Julia thought they would never get there, but at last they were out on the hillside, and there was no sign of the bats.

"I am never going back in there again," Julia vowed.

"I may," Simon was studying the hidden entrance thoughtfully. "A place like this could prove mighty useful."

"I give it to you," Julia told him. "I relinquish all claim to our discovery."

"What if I find treasure?"

Julia reconsidered. "Then you still give me half, but you have to fight the bats for it all by yourself."

"Agreed," he said and boosted her back up over the wall of rocks.

✵ CHAPTER TWELVE

The Boy with the Black Oilcloth Mask

"Someone has been pilfering wood from the school-house supply," Mr. Raby announced. "I have noticed the number of split logs dwindling for some days now, and I have taken steps to stop the thefts."

Mr. Raby was stingy with the woodpile. Although the temperature had started to drop at night and the building was cold in the morning, he still considered it much too early in the year to keep a fire going. Julia shivered. The schoolhouse was drafty, too. She hated to think what it would be like during the long winter ahead.

"I wonder who's been taking our firewood?" Nan asked at nooning. She cast a suspicious glance in Simon's direction but didn't accuse him.

Julia's cousin had started to carry out his plan to "act up" immediately after their discovery of the

100

cave. He'd had another fight with Charlie and been knocked down again, and twice he had been locked in the outhouse, but so far Mr. Raby had not carried out his threat to talk to Cousin Gil. *I suppose Simon might have taken the wood as a prank,* she thought, *but if so, why hasn't he confessed to it? That's what he wants, isn't it—to be found out?*

"It could have been anyone," she said aloud. Then she blushed. Nan and Grace looked at each other and giggled. Julia sighed. Now there would be a new rumor going around. Everyone would say she was sweet on Simon just because she'd defended him.

"I wonder what steps Mr. Raby has taken?" Grace asked.

"A bear trap in the woodpile?" Nan suggested.

Both girls giggled again, but the idea of danger should the thief return troubled Julia. What had Mr. Raby done?

They found out the next day. Mr. Raby was gleeful as he met the Tanners and Julia in the schoolyard. Except for Charlie Kilbride and his sister the other children were already there. "Last night ¬" the wood that was chopped yesterday dis¬
he told them.

Julia stared at the schoolteacher, puzzled because he was grinning happily. She'd never seen him smile before.

"We will soon know who he was," Mr. Raby explained, looking directly at Simon. "I took the precaution of drilling a hole in one of those chunks of wood and filling the hole with gunpowder. When the thief tries to burn it, it will explode."

Julia gasped. She had a momentary vision of Cousin Lucy adding a log to the woodstove in the kitchen and having her whole house blow up. Then she shook her head. If Simon had taken the wood, he'd be owning up right now and gloating because he'd found a way to get suspended from school. Simon looked as puzzled as the rest of them and said nothing.

As the next days passed, doubts began to nag at the back of Julia's mind. Simon was up to something. Several people had been startled by a boy in a black oilcloth mask who jumped out at them and then ran away. There had also been more disappearances. Druscilla Wickes lost two chickens, and some of Mrs. Pargeter's laundry was stolen right off her clothesline—a blanket and a pair of her husband's long johns.

Finally Julia confronted Simon. It was at nooning, but she didn't think anyone could overhear them.

"You've been wearing that silly mask, haven't you?"

He just grinned.

"Simon, it's going to get you into trouble. People are starting to say that the boy in the mask must also be the thief."

"I haven't stolen anything."

"Then who has?"

"You don't believe me!" Simon looked hurt, and when Julia couldn't deny it, he turned his back on her and stalked away.

The accusation hurt Julia, but she did have suspicions. She even wondered if he was angry because she didn't trust him or because he was guilty. She started to follow him, then caught sight of Charlie. He was lurking at the corner of the schoolhouse, and it was plain he'd been watching and listening.

"What do you want?" she demanded.

He chuckled. "What's the matter, Julia? Lose your boyfriend?" Before she could think of an answer, he turned and walked away too. Julia gave up trying to talk to either boy and went to eat her lunch with the twins.

That night there was another theft. Someone broke into the Kilbride house and took all of the money Mr. Kilbride had gotten from the sale of a prize bull. Charlie claimed he'd seen a figure running away, a figure with a dark hood or mask over his head.

Oh my! Julia thought. What if I've been wrong about Simon? She was beginning to think she couldn't be sure about anyone. First her parents had let her down, then Grandmama. She had, she remembered, been wrong about Charlie, too. At first she'd thought him a proper young gentleman, but he'd turned out to be even more crude than Simon was. But Simon didn't steal my journal, she reminded herself. He can't be behind these thefts either unless—she had to face the possibility—his "acting up" has gotten out of hand.

Julia resolved to find out if it had. If Simon was the thief, she knew where he would have hidden the things he'd stolen—the lost Indian mine. She dreaded going there again because she was still afraid of the bats, but a visit to their secret place was the only way she could think of to prove to herself that Simon was innocent. If the cave was empty, someone else was the thief.

Julia brought a candle and matches with her the next day, hidden in her parcel of schoolbooks, and at nooning made her way alone to the hidden cave. She had no trouble finding it, though it was hard to scramble over the rocks without Simon's help.

She paused in the grassy hollow, drew a deep breath, got down on her hands and knees, lit the candle, and shone the light inside. She almost cried. There was a stack of firewood just inside the entrance, and further back she could see the shape of a blanket. She didn't explore any further but withdrew her head, blew out the candle, and sat cross-legged in the shade of the rocks.

This is terrible, she thought. Her worst fears had turned out to be true. If the stolen goods were here, then Simon was the thief. She couldn't understand it. Why had he turned to crime? That had not been his plan. She was sure he had only meant to cause a little trouble when he started out. Somehow, he'd been tempted into going further. He had begun by wanting to appear bad and ended by really becoming bad. Now he could even go to jail for what he had done. Julia wondered if the famous outlaw Charlie's uncle had told him about, Black Bart, had started out the same innocent way Simon had. Maybe Charlie's noontime stories had given Simon the idea in the first place.

Julia returned to the schoolyard slowly, pondering this terrible new development. I have to do something to save Simon from himself, she thought. He's more like the heathens my parents have gone to China to save than the outlaws out west. He's strayed from the path of righteousness through ignorance, but he's not beyond salvation. All I have to do is convert him. To begin with, she decided, I'm going to hide that black oilcloth mask!

As soon as she got home, Julia climbed into the barn loft and felt under the straw for the mask. She found it and hid it in her schoolbooks to smuggle into the house. Her plan was to conceal it in the parlor, where Simon rarely went. Then he would stop his thefts because he would be afraid of being recognized.

Very carefully, Julia pulled out the stitches that

held the material to the back of the horsehair sofa in the parlor and secreted the mask underneath. Then she tucked the sofa cover back into place. There was a slight bulge to show that the mask was there, but Julia didn't think anyone would notice it. Even the dust behind the sofa was undisturbed. This was not a spot many people ever saw.

She was still down on her hands and knees behind the sofa when Grace came into the room. Julia knew it was Grace without looking. She was humming, as usual. Julia stayed where she was. She did not want to have to explain what she had been doing.

It was uncomfortable crouched in the cramped hiding place. The floorboards felt rough under Julia's hands and, as she shifted her position, she ran a splinter into her palm. She sucked on the wound and tried to breathe quietly as she waited for Grace to go.

After a long silence, Julia gave in to curiosity and peeked out. Grace was seated at the baby organ. Very gently, she was touching the keys, as if she could hear the sounds they made in her head. Then, gingerly, as if not entirely confident she knew how the pedals worked, she began to pump the organ. The notes emerged, soft but recognizable. Grace was playing the same tune she had been humming. Somehow, on the organ it seemed more like music.

Grace played haltingly but with growing eagerness. Julia realized that Grace put more feeling into each note than Julia had summoned up in all her years of lessons and practice. Grace had real talent. She was playing songs Julia had never heard before, beautiful songs, and she was playing without sheet music. She had the notes by heart.

Julia wondered if she could crawl out of the parlor on her hands and knees without Grace's noticing. Even from the back, she could sense that her cousin was concentrating only on her music. Cautiously, Julia started to move forward, but the hem of her dress stirred up the dust behind the sofa. Before she could stop herself she sneezed, loudly, twice in a row.

Grace spun around on the organ stool. Reluctantly, Julia met her cousin's accusing stare. She blushed and stood up, trying to think of a reasonable excuse for being there. Grace didn't ask. She thought she knew.

"You were spying on me!" she shouted. "How dare you?"

"I was not!"

"Then what were you doing hiding in here?"

"Nothing!"

"You were listening to my song!"

"I've heard your silly song. How could anyone not hear it? You're always humming it or whistling it. Why don't you just write it down and be done with it?"

Grace scowled fiercely.

"You don't know how to score music!" Julia was

so surprised by the idea that she spoke her thoughts aloud. "You don't even know how to play the organ, do you? No wonder you pedal so oddly. You've never had lessons!"

Grace sprang off the stool, her loose hair flying in all directions. Her eyes were wide and her nostrils flared, and her fists were doubled at her sides.

Julia took a step backward and kept her last conclusion to herself. Grace hadn't had lessons because no one here knew how to play, and Cousin Gil was too penny-wise to hire a teacher. And yet even without lessons, Grace played better than Julia did. Julia wanted to tell her cousin that, but Grace didn't give her a chance.

"I haven't seen you in here showing off your musical skills, Miss Lessons-Since-I-Was-Six-Years-Old!" Grace taunted her. "What's the matter? Are you afraid your wonderful talents will be wasted on us? Are we too beastly for you?"

"You did read my journal!" Julia accused. The idea of complimenting Grace was wiped out by Julia's own anger. "You did steal it!"

"I did not!" Grace was vehement, but she flushed guiltily.

"Liar! How else would you know I used that word? That is what I called you, all of you—beastly! And you were. None of you would even talk to me!"

"I didn't steal your old journal. I found it in

Jeanette's room before Ma did. What difference does it make anyway? You shouldn't have said those things about us. You didn't even know us then. Did you think you were the only one who wasn't happy about sharing a room? I waited for years to get a room of my own, and finally, when Ma put Angeline in with Jeanette, she gave me that little room under the eaves. It was supposed to be a private place where I could go to compose my songs. Then you came along and spoiled it all!"

"I didn't spoil anything! You might have told me what you wanted to do. I wouldn't have bothered you. I might even have helped. I could have shown you how to score music."

"I don't believe you! You'd have laughed at me! It's bad enough you're prettier than I am and smarter than I am in school. You aren't going to get near my songs!"

"I don't want anything to do with your stupid songs!"

They were glaring at each other, faces close together, hands on hips and feet apart, when Cousin Lucy separated them. "Enough!" she declared. "I've never heard such nonsense in my life! I don't know which of you is more stubborn. If you would just listen to each other, you wouldn't have anything to fight about."

Neither girl answered her. Julia was so mad she

couldn't think straight, and when Cousin Lucy sent them off to bed without any supper that only made it worse.

"This is all your fault," Grace accused.

Julia wouldn't answer her. Yet another silent night passed in the room under the eaves.

CHAPTER THIRTEEN

A Letter
from China

October was apple-picking time in Strongtown. Everybody pitched in to help. The Tanners aimed for thirty bushels they could put on the wagon and take to the train and another ten to dry for themselves for the winter ahead.

Julia worked as hard as her cousins and, like them, stopped now and then to munch on one of the large red apples. The skin was thick and the flesh yellowish and somewhat coarse, but it was just the thing to break up the hard work of climbing up and down ladders, picking, and barreling. On one such break, as she rested in the crook of a tree and watched Simon and Grace and the others still hard at work, Julia realized that she was enjoying scrambling up and down the heavily laden trees and stooping for any drop apples the cows had missed. That, as

Cousin Gil had been quick to point out, was one advantage of an orchard of Baldwins. The skin didn't bruise easily. She went back to work with a will, and by the end of the afternoon she saw that she had picked more of the ripe, high-colored fruit than either of the twins.

David was supposed to be packing the last of the apples into elm-wood barrels so that they could be loaded onto the wagon as soon as Cousin Gil got back from town. Early in the morning they'd be taken to the train and shipped to New York, for storage until the merchants put them out for sale after Christmas. Instead, David chose the largest apple he could find and threw it at Daniel, who ducked and returned fire.

"Stop your fooling!" Simon shouted at the twins.

It was not the first apple fight they'd had, and Simon's fuming at them would not have stopped this one either had his parents not returned. The wagon came to a halt by the orchard fence and Cousin Gil got out. In his hand he had a letter and, spotting Julia, he waved it aloft at her.

"From China!" he shouted.

She nearly fell over her own feet getting to the road. Simon had to catch her to keep her from tumbling. Together they hurried over to the wagon, the others trailing close behind.

"Apples all picked?" Gil Tanner asked his oldest son.

"Yes sir, Pa."

"Good. There'll be a dollar for each of you boys in your boxes tonight."

Julia thought she must have misheard him. She and Grace had worked as hard as the boys and harder than the twins for most of the day. She didn't expect to be paid herself, but surely Grace deserved something.

Simon cleared his throat before he spoke. He looked nervous. It wasn't often he dared contradict his father. Julia guessed he was glad Mr. Raby hadn't been to the farm yet, after all, and she was even more glad she'd hidden his mask. There had been no more robberies in the days since.

"Pa," Simon said, "I did more work by half than the twins together. I ought to be paid more."

Cousin Gil didn't even hesitate. "Share and share alike," he said. "You know my rule."

"So do they!" Simon's voice was bitter. "They spent the whole afternoon throwing apples at each other instead of picking. If Grace and Julia hadn't helped, we'd never have finished this soon."

"Share and share alike," Cousin Gil repeated.

"Cousin Gil?"

Julia meant to ask why Grace didn't get a share, but her interruption reminded him that he still hadn't given her the letter from China, and he handed it over. She stared down at it, bemused. She had forgotten too, and that realization shocked her.

This letter was something she had been awaiting for months, and yet now, when it finally arrived, she'd been more concerned with her cousins' problems than with opening it.

Cousin Lucy spoke up for the first time, from the seat of the light lumber wagon. "Soon as the barrels are loaded, get yourselves cleaned up. The Wests and the Kilbrides are coming over tonight for an apple-paring bee."

Cousin Gil grunted and climbed up beside her. The discussion of money was over. As his parents drove away, Simon took off his straw hat, threw it down on the ground and stamped on it. He didn't say a word.

"An apple-paring bee!" Grace exclaimed. "And Nan is coming!"

"And Hattie," Jeanette added.

"And Racie," the twins chimed in, in unison.

Nobody mentioned Charlie, but Julia could guess Cousin Lucy's news wasn't making Simon any happier. "What is an apple-paring bee?" she asked.

"Fun," David told her. "We get to stay up late."

"And eat all the apples we want." David was already munching another.

"You're going to be sick if you keep that up," Grace warned him.

He ignored her. "Aren't you going to read your letter, Julia?"

She looked down at it, reluctant to begin. What if

they'd decided they didn't want her to come to China? She stole a look at Grace. After all the terrible things they'd said to each other they'd never be friends now. Grace hated her, just as Julia had always suspected, and she'd continue to resent her for as long as Julia stayed in Strongtown.

Climbing back up into the crook of an apple tree to read her letter, Julia prayed it contained instructions to leave at once. She ignored the small voice that was reminding her how much she'd miss Simon and the twins and Lefty. She missed her parents too, didn't she?

Julia's perch was a good place in which to think. She could see across the orchard to the farmhouse and the barn and hear the shouts of her cousins as they loaded the barrels on board the wagon; and yet she was alone, shielded by the leafy branches and far enough above the ground to feel apart from what was happening there.

"My dearest daughter," the letter began. "We miss your shining face and sweet disposition more than we can say."

Julia frowned. She knew Mama meant those words, but the letter then went on to tell what a wonderful time they had just had traveling to China without her. Her own journal, Mama wrote, was nearly filled, and she would be sending it to Julia soon.

Mrs. Applebee's letter had taken more than a

month to reach her daughter. It had still been early summer when they took passage from San Francisco, after sitting up on a train all the way across the continent. Then a freighter had taken them to Japan, where they'd switched to a sidewheeler for the trip to China. Julia's mother wrote that they could see a distinct line where the muddy yellow waters of the Yangtse River met the clear sea.

> We went first to Shanghai [she wrote]. We were met by other missionaries and stayed a week to lay in provisions for the winter, because all foreign goods are bought in Shanghai, even our winter's supply of coal. We bought bedding and furniture and food, and loaded everything on junks for the journey inland.

Julia tried to imagine it. They had set out for Hangchow in late August, just about the time that Julia had been starting school. Mama had been glad to leave the city, where houses were crowded close together, even on the banks of the canal. She liked the country better. There the canal was bordered by small, quiet fields, bamboo and willow trees, and little villages full of thatched houses. It took a week to reach Hangchow in the heavy wooden junks. When there was no wind, they had to be pulled by men walking on the shore along a towpath, one end of a rope slung over their shoulders and the other attached to the mast.

Julia sighed. Mama wrote about the mission in Hangchow, too, and how pleasant it was, but made no mention of sending for Julia. It was Julia's journal she expected to see by Christmas.

I'll be staying in Strongtown awhile longer, Julia thought glumly. If only I could think of a way to make amends with Grace. She considered the problem for a long time, but no solution came to mind. She'd already tried apologizing. Grace just ignored her and walked away, as if she couldn't bear to be in Julia's presence.

☙ CHAPTER FOURTEEN

The Apple-Paring Bee

By seven o'clock the farm kitchen was filled with people, and even Julia's spirits were high. Simon worked one paring machine while Cousin Gil manned the other. Julia watched, fascinated, as Simon sat down on top of a board that was fastened to the small machine. By placing it on the chair and then sitting on it he could keep it steady while he placed an apple on a projecting point with a blade above it. Then, when he turned the crank on the paring machine, the blade descended and the apple revolved. In a few turns the apple was neatly pared.

"Here, Julia," Cousin Lucy said, handing her the first pan full of pared apples. "Trim each apple at both ends where the knife of the paring machine couldn't reach. Then quarter and core each one and put the quarters on the kitchen table."

It wasn't long before the table was covered. "Now what?" Julia asked.

"Now the work of the stringers begins." Mrs. Kilbride, Mrs. West, and Cousin Lucy each had a needle threaded with coarse twine. "This has been cut to hang double in those special drying frames," Cousin Lucy told her. The frames were stacked in the corner, each four feet high and made of thin slats nailed to shorter ones, three feet in length. "See those nails driven into the longer pieces of wood? They're equal distances apart, to hold the twine when it's been strung with apples."

"First one's ready," Martha Kilbride announced. She was a fast worker, but the other women weren't far behind. "Charlie, bring a frame."

Charlie had been off to one side, saying nothing and doing nothing, while his mother gossiped with the other wives. Now, with obvious reluctance, he joined the group.

"How is your brother, Martha?" Cousin Lucy asked. Charlie's mother had grown up in Strongtown and gone to school with Cousin Lucy. "It's been several years now since he headed west."

"Not too well," Mrs. Kilbride told her. "He and his partner had a silver mine in Nevada, but they quarreled, and Ned was shot in the leg. He wrote us to ask if Charlie could come out and give him a hand."

Julia looked up from her coring. Charlie sat stock

still by the stove, but the back of his neck was getting redder and redder. She didn't think it was the heat. "You aren't going to let him go!" Mrs. West sounded horrified.

"Of course not."

"No sense him getting shot up too," Mr. Kilbride said.

Charlie didn't say anything, but he was glowering at both of his parents. Julia was certain that if he had had a way to get to Nevada, he'd leave in a minute. She knew just how he felt. She had really believed she wanted to go on to China alone. She was glad now she hadn't tried. Oh my, she thought. Do I really mean that?

Almost as if she'd been reading Julia's mind, Cousin Lucy spoke up. "Julia, dear, share your news with us. What do your parents have to say?"

Julia flushed. She hoped she could avoid reading the letter aloud. "Not much."

"Oh, you must tell us everything," Mrs. West gushed. "Do they find the heathens terrifying?"

Julia shook her head. "I don't think so. They hadn't been there but a little while when they mailed the letter. It takes a long time to get to China."

"Chinamen wear pigtails, and the women wear pants," Racie whispered. "I read that in a newspaper."

"Hush, Horace," his mother said. "Where are they now?"

"They are in the city of Hangchow." Julia gave in to the inevitable. At least if she answered their questions, she wouldn't have to read the letter word for word. "There is a mission compound there. Mama says there are two whitewashed mission houses and a little whitewashed chapel."

Julia described, as her mother had, church services in Hangchow. Men and women separated at the door, and inside there was a high board wall between the sections where they sat. "Mama doesn't mention pigtails, and she says the native women all wear cotton coats with wide sleeves and wide pleated skirts, and they all have tiny pointed feet. They carry their hymn books tied up in kerchiefs, and they all sing hymns as fast and as loud as they can. The first one to finish slaps her book shut, sits down, and ties it back into her kerchief, just as if she'd won a race."

Mrs. West laughed delightedly. "It must be such fun to travel and see strange peoples and places!"

"My parents aren't just travelers," Julia protested. "They plan to stay. Every morning from eight to noon, and again from two in the afternoon until five, they study the Chinese language. Mama says she's been practicing with the gateman, the cook, the maidservant, and anyone else who will listen to her try to speak the Hangchow dialect."

"When do you join them, Julia?" Charlie asked.

She stared at him. His lips were twisted into a snide smile, and the question smacked of deliberate cruelty. He knew very well she was trapped here, just as he was.

"I don't know," she said. The words caught in her throat.

An uncomfortable silence was broken by Mrs. Kilbride. "Do they have music in this church in Hangchow?" she asked.

Julia tore resentful eyes away from Charlie. "The pastor's wife plays the baby organ," she told his mother. "It's a Mason and Hamlin, just like the one in the parlor."

"I didn't know you had a harmonium, Lucy!" Mrs. Kilbride was plainly delighted. "After we finish here, we should have some music."

"Good idea," her husband agreed.

Grace reddened but said nothing, since the idea met with general approval.

The stringing was finished before nine o'clock, and the kitchen was quickly cleaned. The frames were placed against the walls and suspended from hooks in the ceiling so that they would be near the heat of the kitchen fire. "If the apples don't dry quickly," Cousin Lucy explained, "all our hard work will be wasted."

They adjourned to the parlor, where Cousin Lucy had set out the food. There were two kinds of pie, apple and pumpkin, a moist, sweet cake, and cider.

"Do you play, Julia?" Mrs. Kilbride asked.

"A little." Out of habit, she stood up and went to

the organ. Grandmama made her do this too, but it had been months since she'd practiced. All of a sudden she realized how stiff her fingers were. She frowned as she seated herself at the organ and began to play one of the two tunes she knew by heart, Stephen Foster's "My Old Kentucky Home." No one seemed to notice the wrong notes. They all sang along. Then Mrs. West requested a song from the music book, one Julia didn't know. That never happened at Grandmama's house. No one but Grandmama made requests, and Grandmama knew which tunes her granddaughter could play.

"I'll have to sight-read," she said. She began to play, slowly and badly. All those years of lessons had not made a musician of her. She realized all over again, as she struggled with the notes, how much more talented Grace was. By the time she reached the end, there was an embarrassed silence in the parlor.

"Let me play a song," Mrs. Kilbride offered, and Julia gratefully gave up the seat. When everyone was singing again, she crept outside. I've just made a fool of myself, she thought ruefully. I need to be alone for a little while.

Julia stopped in the doorway to the kitchen. Someone else was already on the porch. A dark, silent figure was creeping along the side of the house. As Julia watched, the shadow reached the window to Cousin Lucy's room and began to tug at it.

"Simon, stop!" she hissed into the darkness as she ran along the porch toward him.

But it wasn't Simon. As the dark shape jumped at the sound of her voice, she saw how much heavier he was.

"Charlie!" she gasped. "You're the thief!"

The pieces fell into place the way she could sometimes see the pattern of a jigsaw puzzle—suddenly and with perfect clarity. She had no doubt at all. Charlie, not Simon, was the one who had stolen the wood, and the chickens, and everything else.

"What are you going to do about it?" He came toward her, looming large in the blackness of the October night. She took a step back.

"You robbed your own house," she accused him. Her voice was no more than a frightened whisper.

"So what?"

Julia didn't know what to say. She was too scared to call out. Her legs felt watery, and she wished she had someplace to sit down. Charlie didn't say anything. He didn't have to. She felt the menace as clearly as if he'd spoken aloud. Finally, when she felt she would burst if he didn't go ahead and hit her, he suddenly turned and ran, and Julia collapsed in a heap beside the porch.

CHAPTER FIFTEEN

Mended Fences

It was nearly midnight when the apple-paring bee broke up. No one seemed to notice that Charlie had left earlier, or that Julia was unusually quiet. Just as they did every other night, she and Grace went to bed in silence, but this time there was a difference.

Too many things had happened all at once. There had been the letter from China, and the embarrassing organ playing, and then on top of it all there had been Charlie. Julia didn't know what to do. He was the thief. She was certain of it. Everything fit, even his use of Simon's "acting up" to cover his own crimes by claiming that the robber was wearing a black mask. She had been lying awake for perhaps half an hour when the tears came, unwanted and unexpected but impossible to stop.

She tried to smother her sobs in the pillow, but it was no use. Grace suddenly rolled over and poked her cousin in the ribs.

"Stop it," she whispered, gruff-voiced. "You played better than I could have. At least you do know how to read music."

Julia was so startled that she stopped crying. From Grace, this was nearly sympathy. "But it isn't that," she protested. "I mean, it is, but it's really something worse."

Grace sat up, and Julia did too, so that they were face to face in the darkened bedchamber. "Something about Charlie? I saw you outside. You looked scared to death."

Julia nodded, then realized her cousin couldn't see her. "He's the thief, Grace. I should have had the courage to turn him in then and there, but I couldn't. I was afraid he'd hit me, the way he hits Simon."

"You can tell Pa tomorrow," she said practically.

"I'd have to tell him about Simon too."

"What about Simon?"

Julia drew the covers up to her neck, suddenly chilled. "About Simon's plan to act up in school so he'll get kicked out and won't have to be a minister. He's the boy in the black mask."

"But that'd suit Simon just fine," Grace pointed out.

Julia thought a moment. It would please Simon. That was his plan. It was her own plan that would have failed. Suddenly she felt lighthearted. Grace was right. First thing in the morning she would tell Cousin Gil everything. She smiled in the darkness and reached for Grace's hand. "Will you come with me?"

Grace didn't pull away. "If you want me to."

"I should warn Simon first, and then all three of us can talk to Cousin Gil."

"Agreed," Grace said and yawned. "We'd better get some rest." She snuggled down under the covers, and Julia followed suit.

Cousin Lucy let them sleep in, and it was mid-morning before they awoke. Cousin Gil and the boys were already off in the fields doing chores while the rest of Strongtown went to church. Word came back from services with Nan before they returned to the house. She found Julia and Grace feeding the chickens.

"Charlie Kilbride never made it home last night," she announced dramatically. "He disappeared right off the face of the earth between your place and theirs."

The two girls exchanged a startled look. "He wasn't home at all? Not even there and gone again?"

"Never showed up at all. Poor Mrs. Kilbride's

been frantic all night long. She wants everyone to help look for him. They think maybe he took a fall somewhere and is lying unconscious, or worse."

Simon arrived back in the dooryard while Nan was talking. He snorted derisively. "Probably ran off to join up with that uncle of his, the one who knows outlaws, and chews tobacco, and needs help in his mine."

"You may be right." Nan's snub nose crinkled in thought. "He's always talking about how he'd like to go there, but his parents forbade it. They won't let him near the moneybox for fear he'll help himself to train fare."

"Why don't you tell that to your father, Nan?" Grace suggested. "We'll search here." But as soon as Nan left, she told Simon what had happened the night before. "He's jumped a train for sure," Grace finished.

"Can't have," Simon said. "There haven't been any. First train through Bull's Cut—that's the only place he could get aboard without being seen—isn't for half an hour. Blast, Julia, why didn't you holler last night? We've barely time to get there."

The searchers Charlie's parents had recruited were spread out, covering the fields and forests between the Tanner farm and the Kilbride house. They were to work their way toward a central meeting place at the school. Simon said there was no time to round them up. "You'll have to do," he told the two girls and set off with them toward Bull's Cut. "It's quickest to walk from Strongtown Crossing along the tracks."

They were quiet as they picked their way between the ties, except for the rustle of fallen leaves beneath their feet. Once a rat ran across the tracks in front of them, but they saw no other sign of life. They were almost at Bull's Cut when they heard the sound of a freight train.

"We're too late," Simon said, "and it's coming fast." He pulled Julia and Grace back against the embankment at the side of the tracks. The train went by so close to them that it felt like a hurricane wind. "Now watch!" Simon shouted over the noise. "If Charlie's going to board, he'll have to jump from those rocks!"

Julia looked where he pointed, shading her eyes against the sun. An overhang reached out to within a foot of the top of the boxcars, but no one was there to jump. Charlie had missed his train.

Simon looked puzzled. "There isn't another train till evening, this being Sunday."

"Couldn't he have walked to Liberty, or even the other way, to Luzon Crossing?"

"Not without someone noticing him. He must be hiding somewhere, waiting for that evening train. Darker then."

Julia stared thoughtfully off to the southeast. "I wonder if he could be in the cave?"

"What cave?" Grace wanted to know.

"There's a cave up there," Simon explained. "But Julia, how could he find it? The entrance is impossible to locate unless you know it's there."

"The first day we went, I thought I saw a figure on the hillside. It could have been Charlie. He could have followed us from the schoolyard. Or he could have stumbled on it. Maybe he saw the bats flying out."

"Bats!" Grace shrieked. "Ugh!"

"I think we should go and look," Julia went on. She gave Simon an apologetic smile. "I did visit it once, after the thefts. I thought it was you, and when I saw the wood stacked up . . . oh, Simon! The wood!"

Grace paled. She'd remembered the same thing Julia had. "Charlie doesn't know about the gunpowder in the wood. He didn't get there that day until after Raby told us!"

"And Raby was so sure it was Simon that he never bothered to tell Charlie."

They wasted no more words, but set out together for the cave. Julia felt sick, remembering Simon's story of the boys in Liberty who'd put blasting powder in the anvil. She'd heard more about it later. Hank Hardy had been blinded for three days and still couldn't see right. No matter what Charlie has done, she decided, he doesn't deserve that, and he doesn't deserve worse!

They had almost reached the cave when the blast shattered the silence. The ground beneath their feet shook with the force of the explosion.

"The wood!" Julia exclaimed. "It's blown up!" Then she was running toward the cave, forgetting for the moment that she had a newly mended leg.

Ahead of them a dark shape rose up, then seemed to shatter into a dozen separate flapping shapes. It took Julia a moment to realize she was watching the colony of bats. Her skin crawled, but all the same she was glad they'd escaped. She prayed Charlie had.

Footsteps pounded after her. Simon rapidly overtook her and plunged on ahead. Grace caught up with her next, but stayed at her side the rest of the way.

Julia was getting a stitch in her side from running so hard, and her leg had begun to throb too, but she wouldn't stop. They were almost at the entrance to the cave. Already they could see smoke billowing out from behind the sheltering bushes. The two girls slid to a halt in front of the fall of rocks. Simon was nowhere in sight.

"If Charlie's in there, he has to be gotten out quickly, before he suffocates on the smoke."

"Simon's gone in," Grace said. "We'll only be in the way if we follow him."

Julia hesitated. She wished just this once that she was a boy, wearing trousers instead of her cumbersome skirt and petticoats. Then she had an idea.

Abruptly she sat down and began tearing strips off the offending undergarment. Grace understood at once. They would make bandages.

Together, they kept on tearing the strips of cloth, praying that Charlie was still alive to need them. Julia knew how small the cave was. The explosion might have killed him.

Both girls watched the rising smoke as they worked. It was beginning to thin out, and still there was no sign of Simon or Charlie.

"We'll have to go in. Simon may have passed out from the smoke." Julia put one of the strips of cloth over her nose and mouth and scrambled over the rocks. She didn't know if Grace was coming after her or not, but she threw herself on hands and knees, ready to crawl.

She was about to thrust her head inside the smoking hole when a dark shape appeared through the haze. Julia heard Grace's cry of relief. It was Simon, and he was dragging Charlie after him, but he staggered when he tried to stand up, and violent coughing spasms racked his thin frame.

Julia grasped his sleeve and pulled him out of the worst of the smoke. Then she and Grace wrestled with Charlie's unconscious form. He was unbelievably heavy, but together they managed it, pulling him along the ground by his blackened arms. By the time they'd propped him up against the wall of rock, Simon had recovered enough to help haul

Charlie up and over and roll him on his back on the grassy hillside.

"He's lucky," Simon said, gasping for breath. "He must have been at the back of the cave when the fire reached the gunpowder. There were bits of exploded wood and chips of rock all over the place."

Charlie had been cut in a dozen places, and he had hit his head, but he was still alive. Julia began to bind up the bleeding cuts as best she could. It was hard to see some of the wounds through the blackened skin. Charlie's left eyebrow was entirely gone, and she was pretty certain his right arm was broken. It stuck out at an odd angle at his side.

As soon as she touched him, the boy stirred, groaned, and began to cough. In spite of everything he had done, Julia felt sorry for him. She looked at her two cousins standing over Charlie's body. Already there were sounds on the hillside below. It would be only moments before they were surrounded by the other searchers.

"What are we going to tell them?" she asked.

"He got what he deserved," Simon said. "If he'd known about old Raby's trap, he'd have got clean away with it, and there'd be people still thinking I was the thief." He gave Julia a meaningful look.

"I only thought it was you because the wood was here. Simon, don't you think he's suffered enough? He'll never be able to run away to his uncle now."

Unexpectedly, Grace agreed with her. "It's going

to be hard enough on him when he wakes up, without having to go to jail."

Reluctantly, Simon agreed. "This is what Ma calls Christian charity, I suppose," he said with a grimace. "Next thing you'll both be agreeing with her that I ought to be a preacher."

"Never!" Grace exclaimed, and Julia nodded in perfect agreement.

"If he isn't the thief, then how do we explain the explosion?"

Julia thought fast. "The real thief was hiding things in the cave, and Charlie went in there for shelter because he fell and broke his arm last night on the way home."

"Why'd he light the wood?"

"He woke up this morning and was cold. Agreed?"

"Agreed," two voices answered. The three of them turned together to meet Cousin Gil and Mr. Kilbride as they came toward them across the hillside.

The adults took over. Grace and Julia moved back and let them fuss over Charlie. The two girls sat on the grass and watched. Julia wondered if her cousin felt as worn out as she did. They stayed where they were even after Charlie had been hoisted onto a rude stretcher and carried off, and Simon had gone back into the cave.

"You have soot all over you," Grace said.

Julia looked down at the front of her dress and laughed. Two months ago she would have been horrified. Now she was just happy she had been able to work together with Simon and Grace to save Charlie. "So do you," she said.

Grace smiled. "Did you mean it when you said you'd teach me to score music?"

Julia nodded and realized with surprise that she was looking forward to it. In fact, she couldn't think of anything she'd rather do. "I'm glad I'm here," she told Grace. She still wanted to be reunited with her parents someday, but in the meantime Strongtown no longer seemed such a dreadful place to be.

Simon emerged from behind the rocks. "No evidence left," he reported. "Blown to smithereens." He looked from one to the other and raised an eyebrow. "You two going to be friends now? Seems to me its about time you mended your quarrel."

"He is starting to act like a minister!" Grace complained. "Preaching at us already!"

"Yes, he is. Shall we tell Cousin Lucy?" She stood up and brushed the leaves off the back of her skirt.

Simon groaned. "Two against one. It isn't fair. I'm going back to the farm."

"We'll come too," Grace said, linking one arm through Julia's.

"And it isn't anyone against anyone, not anymore."

Julia slipped her free hand into Simon's. Together they started for home. All mended, Julia thought to herself, and smiled.

❧ AUTHOR'S NOTE

I grew up in Sullivan County, New York, where my family settled in the 1790's, and inherited a dual interest in genealogy and writing from my grandfather, Fred ("Scorcher") Gorton (1878-1973). Grampa penned his memories when he was in his eighties, paying special attention to stories from his boyhood in what had once been called Strongtown. After I sold a short story, "Runaway", based on one of his experiences, I began to see the possibilities for a full-length novel set in the late 1880's.

JULIA'S MENDING is fiction, but Julia's broken leg is treated just as Grampa's was when he was five years old, and fell through the hay hole in his father's barn. Many other incidents in the novel are based on Grampa's memoirs too, and on stories about his contemporaries. The maternal side of my family tree is also represented, contributing both character names and the story of the lost Indian lead mine. My great-grandfather Hornbeck once had a map to it, but he lost and never found it.

Grampa Gorton told me once that he hoped "some noted writer" would one day use his life story. I think he had Ernest Hemingway or John Steinbeck in mind, but I hope he'd be pleased with JULIA'S MENDING too.